Andria Lo

RACHEL KHONG grew up in Southern California
and holds degrees from Yale University and the
University of Florida. From 2011 to 2016, she was
the managing editor then executive editor of *Lucky
Peach* magazine. Her fiction and nonfiction have
appeared in the *New York Times*, the *Paris Review*,
Tin House, *The Cut*, *BuzzFeed*, *American Short Fiction*,
the *San Francisco Chronicle*, and *The Believer*. She lives
in San Francisco.

ALSO BY RACHEL KHONG

*All About Eggs: Everything We Know About
the World's Most Important Food*

Additional Praise for *Goodbye, Vitamin*

Los Angeles Times Book Prize Finalist for First Fiction
Winner of the California Book Award for First Fiction

"Hello, Rachel Khong. Kudos for this delectable take on familial devotion."
—NPR

"A quietly brilliant disquisition on family relationships and adulthood, told in prose that is so startling in its spare beauty that I found myself thinking about Khong's turns of phrase for days after I finished reading."
—Doree Shafrir, *The New York Times Book Review*

"Funny and heartbreaking."
—*The New York Post*

"Khong is a magician, and we are lucky to fall under her spell at the beginning of her brilliant writing life."
—Lauren Groff, author of the *New York Times* bestseller *Fates and Furies*

"Against all odds, Ms. Khong has produced a book that's whimsical and funny. This is because the author, like her guiding spirit, Lorrie Moore, has a love for the ridiculous in the mundane."
—*The Wall Street Journal*

"Strips you down and leaves you feeling more forgiving—and forgiven."
—Stephanie Danler, author of the *New York Times* bestseller *Sweetbitter*

"Incredibly poignant . . . Sneaks up on you—just like life . . . and heartbreak. And love."
—Miranda July, author of the *New York Times* bestseller *The First Bad Man* and *No One Belongs Here More Than You*

"[Alternating] swiftly between quirky and pathos, and a kind of joyous gallows humor . . . Khong displays a deep understanding of the ways in which memory humanizes and connects us individually, communally."

—*Financial Times*

"[A] light-as-air yet powerful debut . . . Khong fuses the poignancy of loss with sharp-witted humor for an effortlessly engaging exploration of family, love, and whether or not any of us every truly 'come of age.'"

—*Harper's Bazaar*

"Manages to create vibrant characters dealing with the same things we all are: the comforts and discomforts of coming home again; reckoning with the people in our lives who aren't who they were, or at least, who we thought they were; grasping at the past and figuring out how it fits into our evolving lives."

—*Bustle*

"Heartbreaking but also funny . . . This isn't melodrama; it's a novel modeled on real life, where humor often rubs shoulders with pathos, and Ruth's gift as a narrator is her ability to observe and record it all."

—*San Francisco Chronicle*

"Wry, warmhearted, and wise, Khong's writing can turn midsentence from really funny to really sad, and often back again. . . . [*Goodbye, Vitamin*] will stay with you long after you turn the last page. What more can be said for a book about remembering?"

—*Vogue*

"Although Khong is indeed writing of a clinical disease, there is a kind of softening—a blurring of reality that allows for a richly layered world. . . . And while the memory loss in *Goodbye, Vitamin* is a vehicle for humor and play, it ultimately is also a means of expressing absolute tenderhearted emotion."

—*Los Angeles Review of Books*

"Though the book is deeply emotional, it's also a playful, hilarious page-turner. . . . *Goodbye, Vitamin* is one of those rare books that is both devastating and lighthearted, heartfelt, and joyful. . . . Don't miss it."

—Isaac Fitzgerald, *BuzzFeed*

"A briskly paced and keenly observed novel of small moments, each one slowly adding up to a surprisingly affecting portrait of loss." —*GQ*

"Reading *Goodbye, Vitamin* . . . is like tasting an entirely new flavor. Gut-wrenching and deeply soothing . . . It's clear that Khong's literary gourmandism is not a shtick but a profoundly affecting way to write about a disease that robs its victims of their past and future." —*O, The Oprah Magazine*

"This slim, wistful book [is] the sort that'll break your heart but leave you smiling. . . . Khong, writing in wry episodic chunks, somehow makes this story never sentimental, rarely sad and ever-surprising. . . . And while a story about a parent whose mind is dimming can't possibly have a happy ending, Khong pulls off something nearly as good." —*The Seattle Times*

"*Goodbye, Vitamin* brims with wry observations and deadpan wit . . . offering a poignant mediation on love, mortality, and memory."

—*Entertainment Weekly*

"[A] flawless narrative and a set of rounded, intriguing characters . . . *Goodbye, Vitamin* is a show-stealer." —*The Independent*

"Khong writes in spare, precise language that surprises in its humor and depth of tenderness . . . [portraying] the imperfect but furious love children show their parents, and vice versa." —*HuffPost*

"Though [*Goodbye, Vitamin*] is remarkably funny, Khong's always willing to head into the storm. Her moral radar is excellent, and instead of drawing humor from her characters' pain, she mines it from the richness of their relationships. Khong also displays an exceptional talent for evoking a lifetime of ups and downs between two people. . . . Powerful . . . Pitch-perfect."

—*Paste* magazine

"A funny and beautiful meditation on family bonds and finding one's place in an ever-changing world."
—*BookPage*

"A good mix of humor and love."
—*Elle*

"In her tender, well-paced debut novel . . . Khong writes heartbreaking family drama with charm, perfect prose, and deadpan humor."
—*Booklist* (starred review)

"Can sadness be sweet? Yes, in the hands of Khong, who turns a swirl of lemons into lemon drops."
—*Library Journal*

"Filled with precise, gemlike sentences, *Goodbye, Vitamin* looks at loss, the minutiae of caring for family or strangers, and the fickle nature of memory."
—*Bookforum*

"Engaging and humorous and deeply touching . . . Khong has created something special."
—*The Charlotte Observer*

"A sparkling and heartfelt comedic debut."
—GoodReads, "July's Best Books of the Month"

"[A] strongly voiced, astutely observed, and emotionally gripping novel."
—*The Booklist Reader*

"A deeply felt meditation on the power and shortcomings of memory. Rachel Khong's writing is smart, funny, and insightful, and *Goodbye, Vitamin* is a total pleasure to read."
—*Chicago Review of Books*

"[*Goodbye, Vitamin*] is both heartfelt and shockingly funny, written with wit, grace, and compassion. Deeply insightful and laugh-out-loud hilarious, Khong tells a late-life coming-of-age story about the impossible complexity of families, the space for humor within sorrow, and what it means to be imperfect and to love imperfectly."   —*The Michigan Daily*

"Laugh-out-loud funny and also full of heart, *Goodbye, Vitamin* is the story of a young woman finally growing up after years of thinking that particular rite of passage was already behind her."   —*Refinery29*

"*Goodbye, Vitamin* is a darkly funny debut novel about love, loss, and heartbreak."   —*PopSugar*

"A spectacular (and necessary) reminder that most answers can be found in our roots, *Goodbye, Vitamin* is a captivating and tender tale about finding stability in life when it only gives you earthquakes."   —*Redbook*

"[*Goodbye, Vitamin*] is suffused with prickly humor and pain, but Ruth's singular voice keeps the book—and reader—from wallowing in sorrow. . . . The result is surprisingly funny, compassionate, and utterly absorbing."
—Google Play, "Summer Reading"

"A quick read that's worth revisiting over and over again."
—*Bitch Media*

"A very funny story of love, family ties, and dementia that manages genuine tenderness while being odd and unpredictable in all the best ways."
—*Esquire*

"Equal parts clever and tender, Khong's *Goodbye, Vitamin* is a moving meditation on what it means to be patient, forgiving, and human."
—Karolina Waclawiak, author of *The Invaders* and
How to Get Into the Twin Palms

"I don't know how she did it, but Rachel Khong has breathed fresh life into the slacker comedy, the family drama, and the campus novel—in wry, swift, spiky, heartfelt prose that is a joy to read."　　　—Justin Taylor, author of *Flings*

"[An] extraordinarily well-written debut novel."　　　*—Goop*

"Poignant and compassionate."　　　*—Nylon*

"*Goodbye, Vitamin* is one of the funniest elegiac novels I have ever read and also one of the gutsiest. It is about so many things—Alzheimer's, fast food, turning thirty, marriage, Southern California, the digestive habits of jelly fish, the invention of the intermittent windshield wiper—and at the same time it is about only one thing, the really important thing: the imperative, as E. M. Forster long ago urged, to connect. Rarely has gravitas been handled with such lightness of touch, or a sad story told so happily."　　　—David Leavitt, author of *The Indian Clerk* and *The Lost Language of Cranes*

"Hard-ball, laconic, severely, even frighteningly, intimate. To boot, a current of food runs through it, a sophisticated but not snobbish celebration of the empiric integrity of all food. The color of Fanta! You will emerge wanting to take a good snifferoo of a fresh radish, to study the underside of a saltine, and, in the face of depression, to be a better and perkier person than you are. This book does it all."　　　—Padgett Powell, author of *Cries for Help, Various* and *Edisto*

"Half stand-up comic, half a seismographer of the human heart, Khong writes with vulnerability and penetrating insight and with a gentle humor that moves you not only to care for her characters, but also to care more fervently for the people in your life."　　　—Alexandra Kleeman, author of *You Too Can Have a Body Like Mine*

Goodbye, Vitamin

❧ a novel ❧

RACHEL KHONG

A Holt Paperback

Henry Holt and Company

New York

GOODBYE, VITAMIN. Copyright © 2017 by Rachel Khong. All rights reserved. Printed in the United States of America. For information, address Henry Holt and Company, 120 Broadway, New York, New York 10271.

www.henryholt.com

Henry Holt® and ⬤® are registered trademarks of Macmillan Publishing Group, LLC.

Designed by Kelly S. Too

The Library of Congress has cataloged the hardcover edition as follows:

Names: Khong, Rachel, 1985– author.
Title: Goodbye, vitamin : a novel / Rachel Khong
Description: First edition. | New York : Henry Holt and Company, 2017.
Identifiers: LCCN 2016039559 | ISBN 9781250109163 (hardcover) | ISBN 9781250109156 (ebook)
Subjects: LCSH: Adult children—Family relationships—Fiction. | Domestic fiction. | BISAC: FICTION / Literary. | FICTION / Contemporary Women.
Classification: LCC PS3611.H66 G66 2017 | DDC 813'.6—dc23
LC record available at https://lccn.loc.gov/2016039559

ISBN 978-1-250-18255-5 (trade paperback)

Our books may be purchased in bulk for promotional, educational, or business use. Please contact your local bookseller or the Macmillan Corporate and Premium Sales Department at 1-800-221-7945, extension 5442, or by email at MacmillanSpecialMarkets@macmillan.com.

Originally published in hardcover in 2017 by Henry Holt and Company

First Holt Paperbacks Edition 2024

D   13   15   17   19   21   23   24   22   20   18   16   14   12

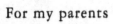

For my parents

Tonight a man found Dad's pants in a tree lit with Christmas lights. The stranger called and said, "I have some pants? Belonging to a Howard Young?"

"Well, shit," I said. I put the phone down to verify that Dad was home and had pants on. He was, and did.

Yesterday, on Mom's orders, I'd written his name and our number in permanent marker onto the tags of all his clothes.

Apparently what he's done, in protest, is pitched the numbered clothing into trees. Up and down Euclid, his slacks and shirts hang from the branches. The downtown trees have their holiday lights in them, and this man who called had, while driving, noticed the clothes, illuminated.

In the morning, when I go to fetch them, city workers are removing the lights from the trees and the decorative bows from the lampposts. One man unties a bow and tosses it to his partner on the ground. All the great bright gold bows are piled in the bed of an enormous pickup truck parked in the plaza.

In that same plaza, a frustrated man is saying to his dog, "Why are you being this way?" A baby in a stroller is wearing sunglasses.

"Dad, all my hard work," I say, later at home. I've collected a pair of pants, two shirts, a few knotted-up ties.

"Now that's unnecessary," Dad says, angrily, when I return them.

I got here on Christmas Eve. I'm *home for the holidays*, like you're supposed to be. It's the first time in a long time. Under ordinary circumstances—the circumstances that had become ordinary—I would have gone to Joel's. His mother would have popped popcorn for garlands and his father would have baked a stollen. His twin brother would have hit on me. In the bathroom, there would have been a new, grocery-brand toothbrush with a gift label on it, my name in his mother's handwriting: RUTH.

This year, with nowhere to go—no Joel and no Charleston—I made the drive down. It's been three or four Christmases away. From San Francisco, where I live, it would have been an easy six hours south. "Up to you," Joel would say, but I always chose Charleston. "Merry Christmas," we'd tell my parents over speakerphone.

Except for Linus being gone, everything was the same. Mom had decorated her biggest potted ficus in tinsel and lights, and with the ornaments we'd made as kids—painted macaroni framing our school pictures, ancient peanuts I'd painted into snowmen with apathetic faces. She'd hung our stockings over the fireplace, even Linus's. When I asked if I could shell a snowman—to see what the twenty-year-old peanut inside looked like—Mom said, sternly, "Don't you dare."

Christmas morning, Dad pulled out a small, worn, red notebook. He explained he's kept it since I was very little. Inside there are letters to me. He'd been waiting for the proper time to share them, but it had slipped his mind—wouldn't you know—until now. He showed me a page from this notebook:

> *Today you asked me where metal comes from.*
> *You asked me what flavor are germs. You were*
> *distressed because your pair of gloves had gone*
> *missing. When I asked you for a description, you*
> *said: they are sort of shaped like my hands.*

Then he closed the notebook, very suddenly, and said, as though angry, "That's enough."

December 29

Now Mom is asking if I could stay awhile, to keep an extra eye on things.

By *things* she means Dad, whose mind is not what it used to be.

It comes as a surprise. Things aren't so bad—Dad doesn't seem any different—on top of which, my mother hates to ask for anything.

"Just the year," Mom repeats, when I can't manage to answer. "Think about it."

On my way to the bathroom, I catch my mother shouting, "No, no, no! You're expensive!" to a vitamin she's dropped. Gingko, I think.

The first things started approximately last year: Dad forgetting his wallet, forgetting faces, forgetting to turn the faucet off. Then it was bumping into things and feeling tired even after full nights of sleep. That he'd been a drinker, Dr. Lung said, didn't help.

There is, presently, no single test or scan that can diagnose dementia with complete accuracy. It's only after the person is dead that you can cut his or her brain open and look for telltale plaques and tangles. For now, it's process of elimination. What we have are tests that rule out other possible causes of memory loss. In diagnosing Alzheimer's, doctors can only tell you everything that it isn't.

What my father doesn't have: hyperthyroidism, a kidney or liver disorder, an infection, a nutritional deficiency. Deficiencies of vitamin B-12 and folic acid can cause memory loss and are treatable.

"I'm just straight-up demented," Dad says.

December 31

This morning I packed an overnight bag, wished my parents a Happy New Year, and began the drive to Silver Lake, to spend New Year's Eve with Bonnie. She's the one with the plans. For the night, I mean. Lately it's hard to make plans at all.

Traffic is worse than usual on the 101, but festive at least. Every window is rolled down. To my right, a tan man in an also tan Escapade has a Christmas song playing. It's the one that starts like the Pachelbel Canon in D and then some kids start singing *On this night! On this night! On this very Christmas night!*

He is *blasting* it, tapping his cigarette out his window to the tune.

For a long time on the freeway I trail a chicken truck that rains white feathers onto my windshield. I try to windshield-wipe them, which only results in their getting stuck in the wipers and moving enchantingly.

Robert Kearns, who invented the intermittent windshield wiper, was legally blind in one eye. It's something Joel told me once. An errant champagne cork shot Kearns in the eye on his wedding night. While driving his Ford Galaxie through light rain, he had the idea of modeling the windshield-wiping mechanism on the human eye, which blinks every few seconds rather than continuously.

I remember absently parroting that fact to Joel years later, forgetting—in that moment—that he was the one who'd originally told me. "Oh really?" he said, as though it was the first time he'd ever heard it. Even now I don't know if he was humoring me or if he'd genuinely forgotten.

The door to Bonnie's apartment is unlocked, so I let myself in. The room smells like toast. In anticipation of me, she's rolled her rug to one side of the living room and laid the Sports section out on the living-room floor.

"Hey!" Bonnie calls from the bathroom, then flushes. "The heater is broken, so I'm running the oven all day," she explains. "Can I interest you in some toast?"

Bonnie is a painter, but lately she makes her living three or four different ways. One of the ways is cutting hair. She won't cut your hair if you've newly been through a breakup. That's her rule. See how you feel in six weeks, she'll tell you, and if you still want the haircut then, she'll do it. But not before.

The reason she's making an exception for me is that, after a breakup, all I want to do is grow a cloak of hair and hide in it. Because she is my oldest, best friend—we met as children, at the college where our fathers taught—she knows this.

"Sit," Bonnie instructs, pointing at the kitchen stool she's relocated to the living room. She snips a neat hole out of the front page and drops the newspaper bib over my head. She hands me a glass of iced tea, which is more for her entertainment than my refreshment: occasionally, I raise the tea to my face, trying my best not to move, and stab myself with the straw.

Divorce Court is on TV while Bonnie cuts my hair. At the end of the show, after the man has not gotten the settlement he wanted, and neither party is very satisfied, he is asked if he has anything to add.

"You still feed me," he says ominously into the camera, addressing his ex-wife. "You still the fool."

What Joel said: that it was not about her. But how do you believe a thing like that, when the facts so unquestionably dwarf the claim? The facts are: the two of them are now living in South Carolina, not far from his family—happier, presumably, than we ever were.

Last June in San Francisco, all our things packed into boxes, I had to caramelize onions in the only clean pan I could find, a cookie sheet. I mixed them in with potatoes I'd microwaved and mashed, and that was our last dinner, though I hadn't known at the time.

We were switching neighborhoods—that was what I thought. I thought we were moving into a one-bedroom in Bernal Heights. I thought we were moving because the space was bigger, and the rent was curiously reasonable. Joel had taken great care to pack his things separate from mine, and I had thought that he was only Joel being Joel, when actually it was Joel not coming with me.

There were signs, I guess, I'd chosen to ignore. At parties, talking to another woman, Joel used to reach out to touch me lightly when I walked by, as if to say, *Don't worry, I still like you the best*. I noticed when it stopped happening. I told myself that it wasn't anything.

Anyway, the point is, I didn't catch on, and what could I have done differently if I had? He told me, *Ruth, don't get me wrong, I care for you deeply.* He said that! And what I thought then—and what I still think now—was, *That's not something to say. That isn't anything.*

"Forget it," Bonnie says. "He doesn't deserve you," she says, sternly, the way friends assure with a lot of conviction but have no way of knowing for certain. What if we deserved each other exactly?

The party is in Highland Park, at the home of Bonnie's friend Charles, from art school. Before it, we drink tumblers of vodka in Bonnie's kitchen and chase them with baby carrots dipped in sugar, the way we used to.

At the door, greeting us, Charles seems nervous or flustered. His face is completely pink. "Does he have a crush on you?" I ask Bonnie, once Charles has moved on to greeting newer guests. But she says no, it's that he's eaten too many Wheat Thins. All Charles had was a niacin flush, from all the enriched flour. It's happened before, Bonnie tells me. The two of them dated, very briefly in college, and that's how she knows. He still loves Wheat Thins. He's still unable to exercise restraint around them.

Inside, a group is assembled in front of a TV that's playing the recorded broadcast of the ball dropping in Times Square. Many of them have familiar faces, but I have trouble placing them. Three or four people, you can tell, have fresh haircuts. I'm relieved it isn't just me.

"Ruth?" one of the familiar-looking people says. He has a thick red beard and ears the shape of paper clips—Jared, my high school biology lab partner. I know—by the unabashed way he's talking—he's forgotten that he was not a very good lab partner. He's a sushi chef now. He graduated recently from a special sushi academy. He has a knack for peeling eels.

Jared asks what I've been up to, and if I'm living in LA, and I tell him, no, San Francisco. But I'm considering staying home for the year, to keep an eye on my dad, who's having "lapses in memory." I don't know why I say that—"lapses in memory." It was what my mother had said, and I was echoing it, because I'd never had to articulate it before.

"Only for the year," I say again.

He raises a punch glass full of something bright blue and knocks it against my champagne. "Cheers," Jared says, full of admiration. It's too much. I excuse myself. I tell Jared I've forgotten something in my car.

In the car, I stretch my legs out across the backseat. I reach gingerly into my purse to retrieve my phone. Gingerly, because my purse is full of trash—so many receipts and pamphlets and ticket stubs I'm afraid I'll get a paper cut.

There's a voice mail from Joel's mother. She's called to wish me a Happy New Year—to see if I'm doing all right. I wonder if it's a drunk-dial. She always liked me—sometimes it seemed she liked me more than she liked her son—and I wonder what she thinks of Kristin. I let myself fantasize that she dislikes her so much that she's had to call to tell me so.

There is, inexplicably, a cigarette in my pocket, where somebody must have slipped it. It's bent and I straighten it and roll down a window to smoke it—it's menthol—while people shout the countdown and the old year becomes the new one.

Joel could be indecisive in a way that exasperated his mother. With him around, I could assume the opposite position. I think she liked that about me. Empowered by his waffling, I could decide: *Let's do this*, and *Let's go here*, and *Are you sure? Because I am.*

Now I think: *I did that?*

My phone rings a minute after midnight. It's my brother.

"I've been singing a song about you," I say, and sing, "Christmas minus Linus."

"It's catchy," Linus says. "You have a gift."

The thing is, I'm not allowed to find fault, not with his litany of excuses, not when so many resemble my own.

I'm wearing somebody else's coat, I realize. I don't know who the coat belongs to—I don't remember seeing a person encased in this particular coat walking in—but it isn't a very effective coat. The owner is probably inside, wearing an impractical outfit. She's going to be too drunk to be concerned about the weather once the party is over. I'm not *sober*, but I am also not drunk enough to be unaware that I'm freezing.

I've never liked New Year's. The trouble with beginnings is that there's no such thing. What's a beginning but an arbitrary point of entry? You begin when you're born, I guess, but it's not like you know anything about that.

A few weeks after the engagement someone asked what I was looking forward to, about marrying Joel, and I thought: *the clarity*. But that was kind of pulled out from under me.

Also, I loved saying the word *fiancé*. Which—whatever. Poor, poor me.

. . .

Back in the apartment, people are kissing at random and Bonnie is on the telephone, probably with Vince, the boyfriend she's been meaning forever to dump, and Charles is still pink, and now also pantsless, cleaning up a champagne spill with paper towels. His pants are across the room, absorbing a different spill. A crowd is arguing about which make better pets, guinea pigs or gerbils, and Jared is halving a Valium.

I finally find my plastic cup, which I've starred with a Sharpie, in a stack of other cups. Originally it was champagne, and now it's champagne swished with bourbon, because my thinking is always, if I'm going to poison myself, why not make it count?

Earlier Jared had said that we were young—*youngish*, he corrected—and that a year was a long time not to be doing what you wanted to be doing.

He was a sushi chef, he'd said, but somebody else I later talked to laughed and said meanly, "*Chef* is one way to put it." This person had been to Jared's restaurant. Jared filleted the fish and pulled pin bones out of salmon, and it was the real chefs who did all the slicing. Jared wore a hairnet on his beard.

And now, even later, back at Bonnie's place, Bonnie and I sit on her balcony, eating peanuts and ranch dressing from a big bowl with a spoon, sharing her blanket. We can hear the parties all around us, picking up and losing steam. We watch the lights blink on and off over the hills across the city.

"You know what happened yesterday?" Bonnie says.

"Yesterday we had someone walk into the salon and ask what the price was for a shampoo and blow job."

"And you gave it to him?" I say.

"She was a paying customer," Bonnie says.

I realize, horrified, that I am wearing Joel's ring. I'd been carrying it in a pocket in my purse. I can't remember putting it on. I jiggle the ring off and drop it back in the purse, where the sea of junk engulfs it immediately.

Bonnie is looking at me, it appears, with fondness.

"Are you," it occurs to me, "admiring your haircut?"

And suddenly, somehow, it is three in the morning and we are back to the vodka and carrots.

"Here's to the new year." I raise my glass. "Here's to new leaves."

"I'm going to be nicer this year," Bonnie says, "but meaner to Vincent."

"I'm going to keep a clean purse."

"You're going to find it in yourself," she says, sternly, "to be okay."

"To being okay!" I cry.

"New year! New leaf!"

"New leaf," I repeat, and we drink.

January 1

Sometimes I like a hangover because it's something to *do*.

This morning's is a rodent: pesky but manageable. The

allergy to Ibuprofen, I get from my mother. From her I've also inherited the tendency to headaches and fevers that do not respond to one *anything*. First order of business, this morning, is two aspirins and a glass of water.

In last night's dream I got caught in the rain. Joel had been holding our umbrella, but he left me. He wandered off to follow a dog that was wearing pants. Fortunately, I was wearing a coat of salami. The rainwater beaded on it and glided off.

I rifle through Bonnie's paintings, propped up against her living-room wall. They're collecting dust and cobwebs, which I brush off with a sleeve.

She drifts into the room, rubs her eyes.

"These are good," I say.

"They're garbage."

"This is beautiful," I say, holding one up: it might be a self-portrait; it's not obviously so. The subject has the same color hair and same color skin and same color eyes as Bonnie.

"Take it," she says, waving her hand, like it's a pair of too-small shoes she has no use for.

Bonnie has funny indents on her face from where her glasses were; she fell asleep with them on. Noticing my hair, she immediately tries to smooth it out with her hands.

"Thanks for the haircut," I say.

"Welcome home," she says, and gives my hair one last admiring look.

At home, my parents are on the couch, clutching tall glasses of pink-orange something. The Rose Parade is on TV. Mom's feet are inside the bottoms of Dad's pants—her way of keeping them warm.

"That's nice," Mom says, about Bonnie's painting.

The pink stuff, it is explained to me, is cantaloupe juice. "I call it 'melonade,'" Mom says.

Mom's quit cooking, like a person might quit smoking or gambling. This is on account of Dad. What she's figured is that it was the years of cooking in aluminum pots, cooking with canned goods, that led to the dementia. She's thrown out the aluminum pots and pans and tossed the tin foil.

She's been reading the online literature on dementia. What she's read: the brain uses minerals to function, and when magnesium isn't available, it uses the next available mineral, aluminum. In large quantities it can cause nervous tissue damage. Though the studies aren't one hundred percent certain.

This is my mother, who once made all our meals from scratch: our sushi, our ketchup, our English muffins. She used to sneak her own popcorn into movie theaters because she objected to the butter from the pump.

This is my mother who cooked dinner every night and— even into high school—never missed an opportunity to pack a sack lunch.

This is my mother, now, who seems wary of everything— who seems to trust only juices and vitamins to do the least amount of harm.

Joel never did like California. He always talked about leaving. Out loud, I'd agree, but inwardly I held out hope he'd change

his mind—that I'd win him over. We've been here forever—
my dad's side, I mean: from Ireland and Germany to New York
and Pennsylvania, my father's great-greats came to San Francisco and Santa Barbara and Pasadena and Palm Springs.

So why not be *here*, in this house where I grew up, and where
my parents still live? I was born in Fontana, the next town
over, on an afternoon in July, thirty years ago. My mom was
twenty-five and newly parentless—parentless *again*—when she
had me.

That same year her adoptive parents were in a car accident
and died; her biological parents most likely continued living,
in China—she had no information about them. Maybe they
thought of her constantly. Maybe they thought of her never.
Maybe they thought of her sometimes, or on special occasions,
like when they became grandparents to children who were not
me. In any case, my mother was without a family. Without a
family but *us*, I mean.

There's a photograph in the living room that hangs above the
piano. It was taken in the hospital, in the hours after I was
born. In it, Dad looks like a hirsute, buffer Linus, with his unruly
brown beard and enormous plastic glasses. He is wearing a
black-and-white patterned T-shirt. You can see the top of his
tight red pants. On a previous doctor's visit, Dad had picked
up a pamphlet titled, "What can my new baby see?" Newborns
have difficulty focusing, the pamphlet said. It's impossible to
know for certain that they perceive color at all. But in studies
they respond to the color red, and to high-contrast patterns.

Next to him, my uncle John is shirtless. Because it's waist

up, he doesn't appear to be wearing anything at all. When John arrived at the hospital in a red shirt, my father was furious at his brother.

"What's the idea?" my dad said, but John, of course, didn't have any idea at all. He hadn't been scheming. He's a colorful dresser because bright colors are always on sale. He was wearing his regular clothes. Dad was beside himself with anger. He refused to let John in to see me wearing the shirt. What you see in the photograph is my mother, stunning despite her eighties perm and with this tired but amused look, my father scowling, and Uncle John shirtless, holding baby me, smiling nervously.

One of the floats on TV is a mechanical turtle, made from moss and sunflower seeds. "It's not the *seed* parade," Dad says, in a bad mood. Mom deftly peels an orange. She opens my father's palm and puts the segments in his pried-open hand.

The bad mood is because last week, Dean Levin called to inform Dad that he would not be teaching this next semester. These past several months, Dad's missed several classes, insisted on another professor's parking spot, and wept in the lecture hall without apparent cause. There had been, Levin said, complaints.

Further "inconsistencies," as he put it, couldn't be risked. My father could have his job back when he recovered, when he could behave himself again. Levin had said *when*, but what he really meant—what we all knew he meant—was *if*.

The floats must be covered in entirely natural materials, the announcer said. Flowers, yes, but also tapioca pearls and cranberries are permitted.

· · ·

My mother hands us each a B-12 pill, which we wash down with celery juice. B-12 builds myelin, she explains, which our nerves need to fire. Celery, a "brain food," contains luteolin, which combats inflammation.

The house is virtually snackless. She's emptied the pantries of foods she's deemed harmful. Everything is a potential cause of the disease. Cereals and breads contain sugar, and high blood sugar exacerbates the disease. Saturated fats raise the risk of the disease.

In lieu of our regular salt is low-sodium salt. We have bananas on the counter and a packet of turkey where the butter should be, and miscellaneous fruits and vegetables for juicing. We have nuts and we have the last shards of a box of Triscuits.

Something Mom does when she's frustrated is she adjusts the arm of phantom glasses on her temple. She got her eyes lasered four years ago, but tonight I notice her pushing at invisible glasses, watching a TV that isn't turned on.

Another reason I know she's not herself: on Christmas, typically her favorite holiday to cook, we went to a buffet. On top of which, she didn't take any baked potatoes for the road.

I read: Alois Alzheimer was the senior physician at the Municipal Mental Asylum in Frankfurt when Frau Auguste Deter was admitted. The year was 1901. She was a fifty-one-year-old woman who was anxious and forgetful and, near the end of her life, behaved aggressively and unpredictably. She died five years later.

Cutting Auguste's brain open, Alois Alzheimer found abnormal protein deposits surrounding her nerve cells. He called them plaques: neuritic or senile plaques. He also found twisted fibers inside the cells: he called those tangles. When plaques and tangles interfere with the normal function of brain cells, that's what we know as Alzheimer's.

The neurons are trying to connect—that's what their function is, that's what they do—but the plaques and tangles prevent the nerve cells from transmitting their normal messages. The cells aren't able to communicate with one another because of abnormal protein deposits in the spaces between them. The cells keep trying and trying and trying, but in the end they're choked off. In the end, they die.

I wish they'd named it "Auguste's." Because, "Alzheimer's"? Really? When she was the one who'd suffered.

January 5

Mom is at book club. Meanwhile it is impossible to get Dad out of his office. Earlier I considered slipping cold cuts under the door. I draw a fingernail on each banana. I rearrange the fruit bowl. Now the lemons are resting on top and the kiwis lurk beneath.

At one point Dad emerges, shirtless, into the kitchen, to

brew himself coffee. I get my nipples from him, I realize, alarmed.

In her absence, Mom has given me two twenties to order pizza—our fourth or fifth since Christmas. The sausage topping looks to be spelling HI, like maybe the pizza maker heard the desperation in my voice and wanted to send me an encouraging message.

Mom's all-ladies book club is reading *Anna Karenina*. Anna's newly pregnant, and I'm picturing all the ladies taking the opportunity to share stories about their own pregnancies. My mother, I know, is probably bragging that I ripped her favorite pair of jeans.

In one of Mom's magazines, there is an article about how to keep your man.

- Never surprise him with short hair.
- Don't try to change him.
- Play games, but not too many.

I catch a glimpse in the window's reflection and surprise *myself* with short hair.

Here's something I haven't thought about in forever. Once, on an afternoon in the third grade, Dad was picking me up from school when we noticed, in the parking lot, a dozen or so hysterical pigeons, assembled on the windshield and hood of another car. We got closer and saw why: there were french fries scattered *inside* the car, on the dashboard. We watched the desperate birds pecking at the glass for a moment, before my father said, "Let's go."

He took us to the nearest drive-through. We bought milk shakes and fries and headed back to the parking lot, where we drank the milk shakes and fed those pigeons, a fry at a time.

That's the memory I used to conjure whenever Linus would telephone to tell me what was going on, whenever Linus said, about our father, *He's a liar, and he's a drunkard, and he's a cheat.* And I would listen, in silence, and comfort my brother, all the while thinking, *No, that's not possible. No, you've got it wrong.*

Linus's deal is that he's angry with Dad. On account of the five-year age difference between us, things weren't the same for him. Linus was in the eighth grade when I left for college, and the next year our father was drinking again. What happened was he hadn't had a drop when we were growing up, and after I left, he did.

In the middle of the night, under the impression I am hearing gunshots, I realize that more likely it's the television, and it is. Downstairs, *Hawaii Five-0* is on TV and Dad is nursing a mug of something steaming. I inquire about it. He's put Triscuits and hot water together and created a sort of Triscuit gruel.

"Hungry?" he asks.

"*Now* I am," I joke.

"Here, take this curved yellow fruit," he says, unhinging me a banana.

"You mean banana," I say, trying my best to not sound terrified.

There is a pause before he says, "I'm joking, daughter."

We watch episode after episode in silence, until somehow several hours manage to elapse.

"Shall we?" I say. "Give sleep another go?"

"I don't go to sleep," my father says, with some indignation. "I go to *sleeps*."

"Good night, Dad," I say, not adding that I know exactly what he means, though I am my father's daughter, and I do.

It's occurring to me that I can't *not* stay.

"Just the year," I'm going to tell my mother.

Just the year is all it will be.

January 6

But first, it's back to San Francisco. There's my job I have to quit, and all the things still in my apartment. I start driving in the morning and reach San Francisco by midafternoon.

First stop is the Medical Center. My supervisor is in the cafeteria, bent over a tangle of lo mein, looking too young to be a supervisor, and tired like he always does. He likes to use *diamond* as a term of measurement. "Just a diamond," he sometimes said, if we were at lunch together, and I was squeezing ketchup onto both our burgers. I liked that.

This past Halloween, he and I showed up at the same party, in matching outfits we hadn't planned. He was the Burger King and I was the Dairy Queen and—a little bit drunk, newly disengaged from Franklin, who had been distracting me from my disengagement from Joel—I put moves on him. He was having troubles with his girlfriend at the time, and did not refuse them.

"So," I say now, taking a seat in the empty chair across from him. "I quit, I guess."

"Just like that?" he says. He tears open a packet of hot sauce with his mouth. This can't be coming as a surprise. I like my job—I'm adept enough—but I was never anything special.

"Just like that," I say.

He wordlessly tosses me his fortune cookie. He has a policy about eating the cookie first. He insists on eating the cookie before reading the fortune. Not eating the cookie, he believes, voids the fortune. I eat the cookie, to indicate to him that I haven't forgotten.

"'To remember is to understand,'" I read out loud. "That's dumb," I say, without thinking, and right away I regret it, because what if these were actually the words of a famous wise person? Words that everybody else knew about but somehow I'd missed encountering? Maybe Jesus had said it, or maybe Confucius.

I ask him how Christina is doing. Christina is his girlfriend. At Halloween he'd been having troubles with *his girlfriend, at the time*, not his *girlfriend at the time*. When they got back together, after the Halloween incident, it was a relief to us both.

"We're looking for a place together," he tells me. "Something month-to-month. She's afraid to sign a one-year lease."

"What's so bad about a one-year lease?" I say.

"That's what *I* said."

"Here's what you do," I say. "You say, 'Let's get married,' and wait a moment before you say, 'Just kidding! Let's sign a one-year lease.' 'Let's have five kids. Let's sign a one-year lease.' "

"Let's move in with my parents. It'll save on rent," he says, catching on. "Let's sign a one-year lease."

"Let's adopt a child from Korea."

"Let's sign a suicide pact."

"No? How about a one-year lease?"

"See you next year?" he says.

"See you next year," I agree.

The light coming in through my apartment's bay windows would be pretty, except all it does is illuminate the dust on the floor. I never fully committed to unpacking. I feel not even the slightest attachment to this apartment.

I fill a big suitcase with as many clothes as it will take, and the rest of the clothes I throw into a garbage bag for the Goodwill. I pack one box and then two more and when it still seems I have not made a dent in my belongings, I decide to trash the rest.

For example: the jar of old almonds on my desk. I like to collect those almonds with the slight curve, the ones that hold your thumb. And not only the curved nuts, but also the nuts that don't have the standard tear shape, that are shaped more like buttons, with a rounded edge instead of the point. Almond anomalies.

What a ridiculous person I am. I unscrew the jar and tip as many anomalies as will fit into my mouth. They're stale and it hurts to chew. I give myself the hiccups.

For example: ticket stubs to movies Joel liked more than I did. His spare car keys. A receipt from the airport drugstore from when, the morning after a red-eye, I bought mascara to wear in an attempt to look less tired. (Joel was picking me up. In the end I looked worse.) Seeds, from the one time we broke our own rule and shared an apple in bed.

It was grotesque, the way I kept trying to save that relationship. Like trying to tuck an elephant into pants.

I put the guitar I never play anymore on the curb. I sweep and mop. I hear somebody pick the guitar up and start strumming a Simon and Garfunkel song.

The doorbell rings. It's Maxine Grooms, MD, here to help with the furniture.

"Way to say goodbye," Grooms says, unhappily.

"I'll miss you," I say, and hug her tightly.

Grooms was the one who happened to be around when I'd caught her—and myself—off guard, by crying, after a fight with Joel, one week near the end. We'd always been cordial, but, at that point, we couldn't have exchanged more than ten words.

What could we have in common? was what, I'm sure, the both of us had thought.

She is ten years older than I am. She wears tall high heels with her doctor's coat; she wears expensive glasses and the perfect, complementary shade of lipstick. She appears flawless and smells amazing, always. Patients respect her implicitly.

We were at work and I was waiting for the handicapped stall that she was coming out of, and she could've simply left me, looking sad and red as a tomato, but she didn't. She stood next to me outside the bathroom and gave my back a few awkward pats.

We had no choice but to become friends after that.

Now we are having a last dinner together, at the Spaghetti Shack—a dinner I'm buying because I feel responsible, because it was my fault, our becoming friends.

That's what I think, sometimes: Who is to *blame* for this friendship?

After spaghetti, after wine, we tipsily drag my mattress to the curb. Within the minute, we watch a man in a Buick pull up. He pushes the mattress onto the top of his car—doesn't bother tying it down or anything—and drives quickly away.

Four years ago Grooms had been married, and two and a half years ago her husband had left her for his barista, who was younger but less pretty and less smart, and last year the divorce was made official.

"But there are days now," was what she said, after she found me crying in the bathroom, "I wake up and it's like none of those ugly things ever happened."

"You're the doctor," I said. "What's your prescription?"

Try not to feel too shitty, was her main piece of advice. Stop, always, at 2.5 drinks. Make a list of good things—however small. I did everything she said. Granted, I would have tried anything.

I often wrote 2.5 in Sharpie, on the back of my hand, nights before I went out—a reminder.

I bought a notebook and started keeping a list.

- Found a ten-dollar bill in the back pocket of jeans from the thrift store.
- Found a parrot-shaped leaf.
- Watched a woman reach her arms overhead and stretch in a satisfying way.

"I didn't want to show you this," Grooms says, "because I didn't want to jinx it. But it's really, really happening." She pulls a photo from her wallet: the baby boy she's been in the process of adopting. He's a miniature Michelin Man. His name is Kevin.

Soon I'm asking Grooms: "Do I say goodbye to Joel?"

"You've *said* goodbye to Joel," she says. Annoyed. Like, what's your problem—have you learned *nothing*? I'm ashamed to have chased her news with this.

We say goodbye. Or I say goodbye, and Grooms grunts her disapproval, affectionately.

I drive to Santa Cruz, where Linus lives—not bothering to call ahead. He's between semesters, which I know means he'll be home, trying to write his dissertation but more likely watching DVDs borrowed from the library, and cursing when he has to skip over the damaged parts, which inevitably there are.

At the exact moment I pull up my brother is standing at his mailbox. He peers at me, like he's trying to focus on something through the bottom of a glass.

I roll my window down. "Need a lift?"

"Nope," Linus says, not skipping any beat. "No thanks."

"You're going to leave me all alone," I say, "down there? With those people?"

He takes a good long look at his mail.

Ten years ago—Linus was a junior in high school, and I was away at college—our father took up with another professor at the school. She taught physics. It had gone on for six months when our mother found out—they were never very scrupulous—after which there were apologies and there was counseling. The professor moved away, and that was the end of that.

My parents never broached the subject with me. Over the phone, they kept conversation light. It was Linus who relayed the goings-on—how strained their relationship had become, how miserable my mother seemed, how helpless. He chose her side easily. The whole thing caught me by surprise—still surprises me.

Anyway, the point is: Linus sees things differently.

Inside his apartment, on his couch, sit neat towers of clean, folded laundry; Linus moves them.

His girlfriend, Rita, is a flight attendant. She's often gone, and isn't home now, either.

"Alaska," Linus says, without my asking. Also without my asking, he hands me a beer and deftly fashions a trail mix out of little airplane pretzel and peanut packets. He empties them into a bowl.

He makes the bed for me with a flat sheet and airplane pillows; he brings me a blanket. He opens the medicine cabinet, where there are sample sticks of deodorant and spare toothbrushes and flat, dehydrated sponges for taking on trips: the sponges save luggage space. They expand on contact with water. He says I'm welcome to use anything, which moves me.

"How is he?" Linus says, finally. This is after three beers. He's put his library DVD of *One Flew over the Cuckoo's Nest* on TV. He asks the question while juggling the socks he's rolled into balls. I know it's a hard question for Linus to ask. The socks mean he can't ask me straight. I want to dignify it with a response befitting the courage he's mustered, but all I can manage is, "He's fine." Linus knows what I mean: that he's his stubborn self—unwilling to accept help.

After the movie ends, we change the channels. On one, a woman has buried herself beneath her belongings. All around her there are cartons of expired things she can't bear to throw away, and a flattened cat.

"Can't you come home?" I say finally.

"I've *been* home," is what he says.

And we let the silence hang there between us—not uncomfortably. He refills the pretzel-and-peanut bowl.

At some point we fall asleep, the both of us, children nestled among the laundry.

Linus makes us thermoses of coffee in the morning and we take them to the beach, where the sky is gray and the ocean is gray and it feels like being wrapped in a newspaper. Seagulls are squawking; the gutsy ones come close and give us piercing stares. They look like Jack Nicholson.

"He's our dad, though," I say.

"And I don't give a shit," he says.

He sends me off with peanut packets. I get on the I-5 and keep the window mostly rolled down and try to breathe deeply, like Grooms always says I should. But all I can smell is hamburgers, or cows on their way to becoming hamburgers. *America.*

My car is completely flush with belongings. I can't see anything in the rearview mirror and this is causing some distress. I cut west, to the 101.

I pull over often. I buy a bag of oranges from a man under a rainbow umbrella. I buy lemons from another man a few miles down. I pocket some rocks at Moonstone Beach, and a couple there asks, in French accents, if I have a steady hand. After I tell them, "Not really," they hand me their camera anyway.

A truck is carrying a wind turbine that looks immense, like a whale.

Another truck, all black, says EAT MORE ENDIVE. It pulls over to let me pass, and the trucker gives me a small wave as I do.

At a rest-stop gift shop, I buy a pencil topped with an eraser shaped like an orange and ask the employee how California came to be known as the Golden State. Was it because of the gold rush, or because of the sunshine, or because of the oranges?

"I'll have to ask my manager," the employee says, hurrying off. I don't stay to learn the answer.

I pull over to get a coffee at a Chevron in San Luis Obispo. The endive truck is parked there, and the trucker is outside, sitting on the curb, eating a waxed paper–wrapped apple pie. He has wavy gray hair and is wearing a Harley-Davidson shirt.

After taking a sip, I cough the coffee onto the sidewalk. My standards for coffee I consider the lowest of low. Meaning this stuff is impossible.

"I meant to warn you about that," he says, finishing the pie.

He tosses me a tiny bottle containing, it says, five hours of energy and an astonishing amount of B vitamins. He says the feeling you got from it was like the sun coming up in your head.

"That sounds nice," I say.

"Nice," he says, "is the goal."

I used to have scruples about accepting drinks from strangers. Not so much anymore. I take a seat on the curb next to him.

"They're a trippy little veggie," he says, about endives. "You grow them in the dark." He pronounces endives "ON-*DEEV.*"

There is a couple also outside the Chevron, standing by the trash can: the woman is voluptuous and the man is ruler thin and they are in their forties or early fifties. They talk quietly together. He is leaning into her, and only their stomachs are touching.

"Vegetable jokes," he says. "It's all I'm good for anymore."

"What do you mean?" I say.

He points to the couple. "Isn't it *romaine*-tic?"

He takes my empty energy bottle in his hand, which is holding his own empty bottle. It reminds me of church with Joel and his family at Christmas; how, after communion, Joel would take the little plastic cup that had contained the blood of Christ, and stack my cup with his. His hand would brush mine when he did, and I would feel like I was in on something.

When the trucker gets up to throw our small bottles away, I notice, for the first time, the back of his shirt, which says, "If you can read this, the bitch fell off."

"I like to ride a bike," he says, when he turns around and sees that I've glimpsed the print on his shirt. "What do you do?"

"Sonography," I say. "Ultrasounds."

"How is it, working with the whales?" people tend to ask.

"Sonography," I usually have to repeat. "Not sonar."

"Are they really as friendly as everybody says?" they'll continue.

I started reading about echolocation so I could field the questions. The answer to "Are whales friendly?" is "Most are." The "melon," which is what you call the fatty organ in the whale head, serves an important function in echolocation.

But the trucker only says, "Good."

He reminds me of my father. They could be the same age. He sticks his cigarette in his mouth and puffs while he engages both hands to rummage in the inner pockets of his jacket. He hands me a small paper booklet. On the cover of the booklet is a photograph of him, looking somber, and beneath it: *COOKERY BY CARL*. I open the book. It's recipes. The first is for endive boats.

"Someone told me it's a tradition they have in Thailand," he says. "Over there the thing to do before you die is compose a cookbook. That way, all the guests at your funeral get to depart with a party favor. Somewhere along the line you can crack this open, see"—he opens the book, at random.

"Say you want to cook trout en papillote for dinner. Well, you're in luck, because there's a recipe right here. So you get your trout en papillote and as a bonus you remember your old friend Carl, too."

"That's a nice tradition," I say.

I make a motion to hand the book back to Carl and he pushes it away.

"That one is yours."

"But here you are, alive," I say.

"No sense denying that you and I will one day both be dead."

He stands up.

"Hopefully me before you," he says.

He shakes my hand.

"A real pleasure," he says.

I drive past billboards advertising pistachios, the lowest-fat nut, and Merry Cherry stands, with their painted grinning cherries, until the furrows give way to desert, and the desert gives way to the roller coasters in Valencia, and the mountains before Los Angeles.

Upland is shaded and quiet and, by California standards, old. On a clear day, which is most days of the year, there's this very blue sky and the San Gabriel Mountains, which includes Mount

Baldy, the highest point in Los Angeles County. It's a picture-perfect postcard picture; it looked, I thought, growing up, exactly like one of those posters you affix to the back of fish tanks.

That's not exactly the truth. I used to think that every fish tank's backdrop actually *was* a photograph of these specific mountains. That other mountains existed didn't dawn on me until embarrassingly late in the game.

My street smells cold and familiar. All the grapefruits are hanging from trees like ornaments. It feels like there's a sun going down in my head, and outside it is rising as I pull into town, my five hours of energy coming to a not-unpleasant close. On our street there is a squirrel that's been hit, not freshly, and now looks like smashed cookies.

"Ruth," says my mother, there to greet me, in the lit driveway of our pink house. I'd forgotten the exact color. It's the color of a cut, ripe guava.

"Hi, Mom," I say.

"My toes are frozen," she says. "Hard freeze. They won't be producing any oranges this year."

January 8

Before she leaves for work in the morning, Mom gives me a lesson in the washer and dryer.

"What you do," she says, "is kick it like this." She gives the washer—which she's loaded—a single firm kick, prompting it to start.

"Some other time," she says, "I'll show you the thing about this dryer."

Apparently, the dryer's deal is that it tumbles, but never with any heat.

Mom retired last year from the high school; now she substitute-teaches. She's been filling in for Mr. Byers, a third-grade teacher at my old elementary school. He broke his leg in a skiing accident. He'd taken hallucinogens. When the snow patrol finally found Mr. Byers, it was inside the deep snow angel he'd dug himself into. He was singing "On Top of Old Smokey."

All day, Dad won't leave his office. I watch educational TV: about how to make Greek salad and chicken potpie, and how to increase the value of your home by painting an ugly brown table black, because as it turns out, an ugly black table is preferable to an ugly brown one. I read ancient newspapers no one has bothered to recycle about improvements in replacement heart valves, prisoners exonerated by DNA evidence, obituaries of notable people I've heard of and others I haven't. I wonder what Bonnie is up to, so I text her. She texts back a photo of a clump of hair she's swept into a pile that sort of resembles a turtle.

There is, in the backyard, a pile of lumber, for the patio cover my father has forever intended to build. The bird feeder, hanging from the cherry tree, is empty, to my surprise. When we were little, my mother always kept it filled. It always attracted regulars, like a good pub.

Every so often, I check the backyard, to see if any birds are dining at the feeder.

Every so often, I take bathroom breaks: I remove my top and examine myself shirtless in the mirror. My nipples really *do* look like his.

I wait and wait for his mood to change, but the birds never come, and the mood never changes.

January 9

He shows me another page from the notebook:

> *Last week I played you the Beach Boys and today you sang the wrong lyrics. You were singing, "I guess I just wasn't made for these <u>tides</u>" and when I tried to correct you, you said, "Well, they were the Beach Boys, weren't they?" You made a very good point.*
>
> *Today you asked about storms, and their eyes. You asked what it was like, to "see like a storm." You asked, with great concern, "What do birds do in the rain?"*

Actually, I remember that.

"They huddle beneath the leaves," I remember my father saying. "Their feathers shed the rain. You ever heard of a birdbath?"

he'd said, when I seemed unconvinced. "Don't worry. They don't mind it."

What else I remember is that despite my dad's answer, I didn't feel very placated. I was worried for them, still. When I questioned him further, he seemed irritated.

It was my mother who helped me build a birdhouse. We built it out of Popsicle sticks. The birds didn't mind the rain, she assured me, but it was nice to have options.

I detach the empty bird feeder from the bare cherry tree. I collect coins from the carpet and put them in my pocket. Later in the day I wash those pants, forgetting to remove the coins. They come out shiny. I call, "Dad?" and receive no response, though I can hear him in there, shifting.

January 10

I shake the sand that's collected on the welcome mat and wonder if the saying "To wear out one's welcome" came about because of the mats. Did somebody visit somebody else so often that the WELCOME actually faded? Then I wonder if *everyone* who's ever shaken a mat has wondered this.

I do a load of whites and refill a mug with puffed rice while the clothes spin and stay wet. I fold the white, still damp clothes and eat more cereal and do the darks and listen to the sound of the toilet's periodic flush. Over the phone, Bonnie complains that Vince has lately been leaving his laundry with her.

"And then expecting me to check his pockets," she says. "For joints."

"Remind me how old he is?"

"Twenty-five," she whispers.

This makes me a terrible person, I know, but it comes as a relief to me that my best friend is in a not-dissimilar boat—the unmarried and careerless boat. Which is more like a canoe.

The unofficial plan had been to never abandon each other. Bonnie grew boobs before I did, but we still wore our first bikinis together. We were at Huntington Beach, wearing big T-shirts over our suits. We were fourteen. Neither of us would take her T-shirt off first.

A man on Rollerblades stopped to say hello. He called us *pretty*, which was exciting in the moment, but we'd learn, later in life, that men tended to say that when they found your appearance confusing, when they couldn't tell what you were—when you were half-Armenian in Bonnie's case, or half-Chinese in mine. The man on Rollerblades bought us each large lemonades. When he handed us the lemonades, we gushed *thank you*, so excited, never having been recipients of this sort of attention. Then he pulled out a condom from his pocket.

He asked, "Do you know what this is?"

We looked at each other, looked back at him, and nodded.

"Will you show me how to use it?" He grinned.

We abandoned our lemonades. We *ran*.

• • •

When Dad comes to the kitchen to take a banana, he notices the fingernail I've drawn on it. He seems to notice me, suddenly, too.

He says, "Ruth."

I say, "Dad."

"I'm fine," he tells me.

"I know," I assure him.

"I told you I'm fine," he repeats, annoyed. "Why don't you go home?"

When Mom gets back later she says, "Howard, don't be like this," standing outside my father's closed office door.

"Irascibility is common," Dr. Lung had told us. "It is, unfortunately, unpredictable. There might be stretches of confusion, followed by days when he seems nearly back to normal."

"I'm not hungry, Annie," comes the reply.

She slips a pizza slice underneath the door, giving me a conspiratorial look as she does. It gets pulled in.

Alone at night in San Francisco, after Joel left me, awake with worry about something or other—like getting diabetes or having an embolism—after it was too late to call Grooms to describe to her my symptoms, I'd hear the building sigh, like it was disappointed. I'd hear my upstairs neighbor, Mr. Deforest, turning over in his bed. And then there were the sirens, the car alarms, the city noises.

Here it is so, so quiet.

Today a man calls the house and introduces himself as Theo, my father's teaching assistant. I start to ask if he could please hold, when Theo interrupts and says, actually, it isn't Howard he wants to talk to—he's called hoping to talk to *me*.

He and a few other master's students want to meet for a class, he tells me. It wouldn't be a real, for-credit class, but Dad wouldn't have to know that part. Theo normally took care of the administration, anyway. Everybody else would be in on it: the students wouldn't get credit, of course, and they were fine with that. It would be a way for my father to continue teaching, stay occupied, keep his mind off, well, losing it.

"We could meet on campus, say, once a week," Theo says. "Howard would continue teaching as usual. As for the administration—well, there's no reason Levin or anybody else higher up has to know."

"Hang on. So you're suggesting that my dad teach a class"— I'm processing this slowly—"that isn't real?"

"Except that *he* won't know it's not real."

"We'd lie to him."

"It won't be a legitimate History Department class," Theo says. "In all other ways, it'll be a class. He'll teach; we'll learn. He *wants* to be teaching. That's obvious to anyone."

"Yeah," I admit.

"None of this sounds easy for him, and trust me when I say we'd all like to help him out here."

What's the harm? is Theo's argument.

I ask why the students would voluntarily attend a class that offers no credit.

"Because we all care about him," he says. "Your dad's a good teacher. And a good friend."

Which shouldn't come as a surprise, of course, but does.

To me, his being a good or bad teacher didn't matter: what I remember are those afternoons Dad was in charge of Bonnie and me—those afternoons he lingered over his work, while we wanted so badly to be elsewhere. *One more chapter*, he would say, barely registering us, while we found ways to entertain ourselves. We'd harvest sour grass outside and chew on the stems; we played Crazy Eights in the one uncluttered corner of his office while the students stopped by, and discussed incomprehensible-to-us topics. I remember a lot of laughing; I remember wanting to be in on it. I stopped tagging along to campus when I started middle school. That's when I was allowed—*finally*, it felt—to stay home to watch Linus.

"He means a great deal to us," Theo reiterates.

Then Theo makes me take down his number. I don't write it down the first time, but he asks me to repeat it back to him, and says "Ha!" when I can't, so I fish a receipt from my purse and write it there.

January 16

I kept a pair of running shoes in my locker at the medical center. Whenever I grew weary—every other day, approximately—

I'd eat a few Falafel Planet falafels and head to Kezar Stadium, and attempt to run myself into a euphoric state. It never worked, but I never gave up—I'd make like a hamster and run. If I was lucky I could run myself into a stupor, which was the next best thing.

Here I jog up and down the staircase, and count the flights like laps.

Eat, I try to communicate to the blue jay that's hopping on the arm of our lawn chair. It is four hops away from the feeder, which I yesterday filled with sesame seeds, when it flies away.

I take the Christmas tree, with its dried-out needles, to the side-walk. I wanted to see how long I could keep it alive with sugar water. It's fought the good fight, but the tree, it's obvious, is no longer with us.

On *Family Feud*, one of the categories is "Advantages of artificial trees over real trees." One of the popular reasons is "no smell." More and more, I get this feeling I don't know a thing.

January 19

Dinner is take-out enchiladas and tamarind sodas. Yesterday was filets-o-fish. The day before it was rotisserie chicken. To Mom, it seems not to matter that these restaurants most likely use aluminum. She got tired, I think.

Mom and I eat our enchiladas in the living room, in front of the TV, on which Dr. Oz is measuring a woman's calf. This number will reveal her risk of stroke and liver problems, he says.

About the ripped piece of yellow paper hanging from the sleeve of my mom's cardigan, she says, "A glue-gun accident."

When I ask how she's doing, Mom says, "Fine, fine, fine."

What I'm telling her: Aluminum is in cake mix, antiperspirant, antacids. There's aluminum in the earth's crust.

What I mean is: *You're not to blame for this.*

What I mean is: *It's not your fault.*

"Put on a sweater," Mom replies.

I've been taking from the top of my suitcase, not exhuming any farther.

"I'm cold looking at you," she says.

January 20

"Dad? *Please.*" I'm sitting outside the door.

"Go home," he says, for the two hundredth time.

I slide him a tortilla, into which I've folded jam.

What do I do all day? I don't even know. I dig hair out of the bathroom drain with a chopstick. I listen to what sounds like a dog whimpering, and which turns out to be a squirrel talking to another squirrel. I watch a woman in scrubs walk by our living-room window, neatly eating a taco.

I read messages on Alzheimer's caregiver forums—threads about Medicare, about the best brand of adult diaper, about what to do if your loved one accuses you of stealing his money. Consensus: Be calm, apologize.

On a different board, I read the messages about how to find your life's passion. Consensus: Try everything! Be sure to do all the quizzes in *What Color Is Your Parachute?*

How unfair, that he isn't sad—that Joel never spent time mourning us. What goddamned fucking unfair full-of-shit bullshit.

"Ruth," he joked once, "I'm going to change my last name to 'Less' and then marry you." I was never planning to change my last name anyway, so joke's on him, I guess.

January 23

I find Levin's phone number and extension on the college website. Now I'm calling him.

"Hello?" he says, sounding very tentative. I realize it's my father's name that shows up on his caller ID.

I introduce myself, and apologize: *I don't know if you remember me.* The last time he saw me I was probably twelve or thirteen. I remember being rude to him—no ruder to him than anyone else, but rude just the same.

I remind him that I'm Howard Young's daughter, and Levin asks, reluctantly, how my father is.

I tell him: My father has never been better! In fact, that's why I've called! I realize the semester has already begun, but is there any way for him to get his job back?

I'm being as polite as I can manage. I've adjusted the pitch of my voice—it's higher.

After I've stated my case, there's a long pause.

"I'm afraid that's not possible," the dean says.

"Would you be open to a trial period?" I ask, pleasantly.

"I would not," he says.

"But why not?" I persist.

Something like twenty seconds pass.

"Ms. Young," Levin replies, not having any of this. "You understand: your father is unwell. My decision takes into consideration the safety of all involved. I hope I'm being clear." He pauses. "If I see your father on campus, I'll have to call the police."

They'd always had a rivalry, Levin and my dad, but they had always been cordial. Years ago Levin got the promotion that Dad had wanted. I could see why it enraged my father, to be at Levin's mercy. His smug voice made my blood boil.

I call Theo to admit defeat. Not exactly in those words, though.

January 24

At five this morning, while my parents are still asleep, I drive to the doughnut shop. There are two people in line: a stout woman in a short sequined dress buying crullers, and a tall, messy-haired man who looks to be in his thirties, with his hands in his pant pockets. Noticing me, he takes a hand out and gives me an awkward half-wave. His wallet falls out of his pocket in the process; he bends to pick it up, sheepishly.

"Ruth?" he ventures.

"Theo," I say.

Theo asks what kind of doughnut I want, and I tell him glazed. He proceeds to buy us a few glazed doughnuts, a matching number of doughnut holes, and a couple cups of coffee. We settle into a table in the middle of the shop, as though someone might notice us in the window.

The plan is to meet on Mondays, because Levin, our nemesis, isn't on campus on Mondays. But first we need to find a classroom: morning to night, the History Department building is back-to-back full.

"I'll let your dad know that the department changed its mind about letting him teach," Theo says, putting the smallest splash of cream into his coffee with his left hand. I notice a scar, an inch between his index finger and thumb—pale and shiny. And then I notice there are at least four other markings, streaking the back of his hand.

"My cat gave those to me," he says, because I'm the worst at not staring. "I was ten. Anyway, I'll e-mail him with the list of enrolled students."

"Who are the enrolled students?"

"Former students. Grad students who've been in his civil rights class."

"What about his office?"

"I'll tell him it was moved," Theo says. "And that he can use mine."

"Where will you be?"

"I'll share space with my friend Joan," he says. "It's only a semester. It's no big deal."

He chews a doughnut hole. "I feel like I have to buy the holes," he says, "because doughnuts have their holes punched out of them. Whereas bagels' holes are made by stretching. Not buying them feels like being part of the problem."

All the doughnuts are gone and I can tell he's trying to decide whether or not to say more. I attempt to take a drink from my empty coffee cup.

"He was sending these e-mails," Theo says.

E-mails to the provost insisting that Levin be dismissed. List after list of his shortcomings, one after another, and the president had mentioned some of these complaints.

So Levin was none too happy about it.

But that aside, the myriad grievances were true—things had been slipping. Dad had mixed up dates—shown up for Thursday classes on Fridays, Wednesday classes on Mondays. He'd left classrooms of students waiting. Forgotten names. Forgotten tests. Forgotten grades.

"He seems okay," I say.

"He seems okay," Theo agrees.

"Hey," I ask. "How'd you know I'd be home? You know, when you called?"

"Your dad," Theo says, "talks about you all the time. He was so excited that you were coming home for Christmas." I have to look away, embarrassed.

At home I save Theo's number into my cell phone and give him a code name: PHILLIP. I throw away the receipt that I've writ-

ten Theo's number on. It was from years ago—for a meatball
sub and a Coke I shared with Joel in the cafeteria. I remember
Joel had been in a good mood, and it had helped to buoy mine.
That morning I'd had a woman scream at me. In her ultrasound
photo, it looked as though her baby didn't have a foot.

"YOU SAID SHE WAS NORMAL," the woman shrieked.

I tried to point the foot out to her, but it was too little too
late. The woman was already inconsolable.

"She should be fired!" she'd screamed to everyone, storming
out of the exam room while pointing damningly at me.

And even though my coworkers laughed sympathetically
about it afterward, and even though this patient was known to
be a drama queen, and even though Joel said, "You can't let that
get to you," I couldn't help it—I let it, anyway.

January 26

When I call Dr. Nazaryan to tell him the idea, he seems
unperturbed—even excited. He says it so happens he's actually
rescheduled his Monday seminar, so we can use his classroom
for our first meeting.

"Have you seen Bonnie?"

"I have."

"I'm glad to hear you're in touch again," he says, gently.

"I'm glad, too," I say.

January 30

"They changed their minds?" is Mom's reaction to Dad's news about the semester of class he's going to be teaching after all.

She is pushing an iron down the sleeve of one of Dad's dress shirts. The smell of ironing is a smell I love. The iron travels down the sleeve, like a ship on a shining river.

She says nothing for a moment. She glances at me—my face is doing I don't know what. Suddenly, she gets it. I see her decide not to object.

"Take Ruth with you," Mom says.

"It's work, Annie," Dad replies, avoiding my gaze.

Mom's looking at him in a funny way. It's pity, I think— possibly even disdain. It's two seconds, maybe, then passes.

"Please, Howard." Mom touches his upper arm. "Maybe she'll learn something."

"Can you assist?" Dad says, skeptically.

"I'm a professional assister," I say. "I'm at your service." I salute him.

Reluctantly, he tells me my duties: I am to make sure that the library has the textbooks the students need. I am to photocopy the materials that aren't available in book format, and get them bound.

"Can you handle that?" Dad asks. I tell him I can.

February 2

We drive to campus, Dad in his ironed shirt and a shiny tie. He always used to point out the types of trees to me. He points to one now and looks at me expectantly.

"Holly oak," I ID.

He points at another, a crape myrtle. There's a southern magnolia, and a California pepper, which is my favorite—knobby with drooping leaves like a willow's.

Barring two exceptions, there is no such thing as a native California tree, he says to me, in his teacher's voice. It's because of him I already know this. All the trees in California at some point were carefully selected, then planted, coaxed into growing here.

Except for redwoods. The other exception: ancient bristlecone pines, the oldest trees in the world, which somehow live in California—in Bishop. The oldest one is five thousand years old, and its location is a Forest Service secret. It's in Bishop, and that's all the public can know. We can't be trusted.

Dad's parking permit has expired, so we park in the visitors lot.

"Make yourself useful," he says, peeling the permit sticker off and tossing it at me. "Renew this thing."

"I'll look into it," I lie.

We meet in Dr. Nazaryan's classroom where, sitting around a conference table, are eight students. The room is small with a powdery chalkboard in front and fluorescent lighting overhead. He greets each by name, then introduces me and says I'll be helping this semester. They all call him Howard.

. . .

Dad says: This course is California History, Pre-European Contact to the Present.

We'll cover the Spanish arrival in California, the hide-and-tallow trade, the Mexican-American War, the gold rush, the building of the railroads, the San Francisco earthquake, the importance of water: the rise of Hollywood and the failing of the St. Francis Dam.

We'll touch on California's environmental diversity and abundant—seemingly inexhaustible—natural resources. Immigration, agriculture, and so on. I hand out photocopies of the syllabus.

Actually, I never finished college. Joel was two years ahead and had been accepted to med school in Connecticut. *I miss you too much*, he said, on one of our phone calls, during the long-distance year—a thing I took, and ran with.

I'm flattered too easily, is my problem. One of them, anyway.

This is why a person would, seven months shy of finishing college, decide to drop out. I'd had pretty good grades.

In Connecticut, I got a job cutting fabric at the Discount Fabric Outlet, where mothers would come to buy the fabric to sew their kids' Halloween costumes. I could still tell you what fabric to buy to outfit a reptile, or a Power Ranger. Six months of that, and then I enrolled in my associate's program. Then Joel's residency took us to San Francisco, where we both got jobs at the medical center.

And I liked it. It seemed like fate: a roundabout route to your happy career, and I did, I did like it. It seemed romantic.

After class, outside the seminar room, students linger. Someone says she read it was safe to eat cows with eye cancer. Someone else says that in Chicago, where it is twelve degrees below zero, a peacock was found frozen to a pine tree. A biplane is flying overhead: toward sunset, west.

"Theo, my daughter," is how Dad introduces me.

Theo, who's wearing the same crumpled shirt he wore to the doughnut shop, sticks out his hand and says, "Pleasure to meet you," very coolly. We shake hands like perfect strangers.

Across the courtyard, Dr. Nazaryan is hurrying somewhere and carrying a briefcase that appears to weigh him down on one side. He waves hello.

They're serious about their fountains on this campus, and as kids, so were Bonnie and I—tossing in dimes and quarters whenever we had them. We'd pull connected pine needles apart like wishbones. I don't know how we came up with so many wishes; I can't remember a single one. But what could we have wanted back then?

We never shared those wishes. We were scared that by sharing them, they wouldn't come true. But now it occurs to me that if we'd divulged them to each other then, we'd be better able to remember them now: we'd have someone else to help with half the work of remembering.

Summer afternoons, one of our dads would pick us up from our day care and seat us in the back of their afternoon classes. We'd whisper and wriggle through the two hours. On the days it wasn't too hot out, we would lie out on the lawn with our fathers' students, who found us funny: their professors' strange little girls. What I remember are the days when there were clouds, when they'd try to get us to see shapes. We were always disappointing them, I think. Clouds looked like scrambled eggs to me.

"Cotton candy," Bonnie would suggest, not helping.

"Ground beef?" I'd try, and they wouldn't be pleased with that answer, either.

"But what *else*?" they'd persist.

My parents don't have a clue that I didn't graduate. I had to lie to them only barely. I told them I didn't want them to fly all the way to see me walk—the ceremony would be silly and expensive. I told them I'd been mailed my diploma. They had no reason to believe otherwise, and they didn't insist, because I so vehemently out-insisted them.

I try not to make a habit of playing out the possibilities: if I'd finished college, I'd have been this or that, or something else. It's a game I try not to play because it doesn't end any way but the way that it does—the way that it has.

It was idiotic of me not to finish school, though. Idiotic, and stupid, and now what?

February 5

There's a lone page on the kitchen counter.

> *Today you had me excavate your nose, which you'd*
> *put corn into.*
>   *Today, while I was trying to teach you to swim,*
> *you asked how deep the pool was. When I said four*
> *feet, you looked incredulous, and said, Whose feet!*
>   *Today we went over to your mother's friend's*
> *house for dinner. We'd asked you to be polite, so you*
> *said, "No more, please, it's horrible thank you."*
>   *Today was my birthday, and you asked me how*
> *old I was. When I told you thirty-five you seemed*
> *stunned. You asked me if I started at one. Then you*
> *asked: When do we die?*
>   *Today you said, apropos of nothing, "Good*
> *corpse, bad corpse."*

February 7

Bonnie and I are lying on Vince's little black couch, in his little
adobe house in Highland Park. I can count the number of
times I've hung out with Vince on one hand. Right now is the
fourth. Vince, whom Bonnie has dated for the past three years,
is tan, compact, and doesn't read the news or eat anything with
legs. He will sometimes press eyedrops into his eyes while he's

talking to you. At some point I stopped judging friends' boy-friends, because who knows? But even Bonnie is aware of Vince's ridiculousness.

His Boston terrier is chasing a rolling Pringles tube across the carpet. Vince is in the kitchen cooking and telling us, "If you're a sled dog, and you need to take a shit, you *just do it*. The other dogs drag you along. While the shit's falling out of you!" A few moments later he emerges from the kitchen and presents a stir-fry.

"This is good," we say.

"I've had Chinese girlfriends," Vince says, and beams, proudly.

February 8

In the morning, from Bonnie's, I make my way to Uncle John's. He lives like an obdurate bachelor, on the same acre of land in Tehachapi where he's lived since I was a teenager. There's a shooting range and a little decorative koi pond with an elegant and healthy population of fish. He likes to feed them good bread—nothing Wonder.

His golf cart isn't in its regular spot when I arrive so I trek to the range, where he's been shooting a happy face into a water-melon. When he sees me he doesn't put the gun down imme-diately. I approach when he's through. He's shot angry eyebrows into it.

He hands the padded vest to me and lets me shoot a few. He launches some strange skeets and when I shoot them they make a funny noise. He reaches into his pack, holds up what looks like a hardened biscuit.

"The biodegradable skeet," he says. "This is how I'm going to make my millions."

He cooks lunch: mackerel buried in salt and wrapped in aluminum foil and baked. He roasts lemon wedges. We squeeze juice from the browned lemons over the fish.

I remember when I was eleven or twelve, on a camping trip, Uncle John cooked Linus and me a trout we'd caught, over a fire, and we ate peaches from a can, and nothing—it seemed—had ever tasted and would ever taste so good.

"Foil," I say now. "Didn't you get the memo about foil?"

"Your mother is nuts," he says.

I ask if he remembers the time she tried to make Cheetos from scratch. I was nine or ten and Cheeto obsessed. She drove us two-plus hours to the Frito-Lay factory in Bakersfield, where we toured the plant in hairnets and shoe covers. At the end of the tour, we sampled the freshly manufactured Cheetos, still warm from the industrial process they had undergone. A few weeks after that trip, she arrived at an actually impressive Cheeto—cheese dusted and craggy.

"Your mother is nuts," he repeats. "But she is the best."

February 9

This is our plan for this week's class: an acquaintance of Theo's who teaches chemistry, another PhD student, is on vacation for the next two weeks. His classroom is open. Our excuse, to Dad, is that last week's classroom is being refurbished.

"It's really outdated," he agrees.

Before we leave for campus, my phone rings. The screen says PHILLIP is calling. I hurry to the bathroom.

"Hi, Phillip," I say, casually.

"What?"

"That's your code name," I whisper.

"Oh hey, uh, Ned," Theo replies.

"Ned?"

"I saw Levin's car in the parking lot," says Theo. "At least I think it's his. So maybe, to be on the safe side, don't park in the visitors lot? And maybe don't walk past the Arts buildings?"

To Dad, I propose dinner at Señor Amigo's. It's a block from school and northwest—Levin's office is southwest—and I can leave the car parked in the restaurant's lot.

Our waitress is a teenager. She tilts her sombrero up to register my father.

"Professor Young!" she squeals.

"I'm Layla!" she says to me.

She tells us about her semester—boring so far, she misses Dad's class—then sneaks us guacamole, magnanimously, and whispers, "Shhh."

After dinner, we walk briskly to the classroom. It's lightly raining so I hold an umbrella over the two of us, low, and usher us hurriedly.

This is what we learn from Dad: The name "California" came from a sixteenth-century romance novel that was popular in

Spain. In the novel, California was a land where Amazonian warriors lived—all women, no men, with beautiful, strong bodies.

When the Spanish explorers arrived in the real California, between the sixteenth and eighteenth centuries, they didn't think the place looked like much: no particularly valuable natural resources—none, at least, that they were interested in. Only trees and mountains, mist and fog—nothing to write home about. They stuck around anyway.

Five minutes before class ends, Theo takes a bathroom break to survey the situation. He texts me that Levin's car, for some reason, is *still* in the parking lot. But he's also not in his office. Meaning he could be anywhere.

Theo text messages all of us with a new plan. We're going to have the tallest students walk Dad to the car, thereby blocking view of him. Theo will be on one side; Jake, who's six two, will walk on the other. I'll walk ahead, scouting.

"But Ruth is a liability," someone else texts.

"Do you have sunglasses or something?" Theo texts me.

The Amigo's parking lot is now full of cars, but I spot him pretty much immediately: Levin is leaning against a silver Camry, sipping from a to-go cup and checking his cell phone. He seems distracted; he isn't looking our way.

Theo slings an arm around Dad and we pick up our pace. Levin's glancing at the Señor Amigo's door, then at his watch, then at his phone. We get Dad into the car successfully.

I'm still wearing my sunglasses. I think Levin notices us pulling out of the parking lot, but I don't know for sure. My heart is beating crazily.

• • •

On the drive home, Dad is chatty. He's happy, he's making plans. He wants to finish writing his book this month, he says. Maybe attend some conferences in the spring.

"Sounds great, Dad," I say, as convincingly as I can.

February 10

In last night's dream, I was in high school geometry class. There was a class pet: a canary who chirped with the correct answers. He'd been trained in square roots. A classmate, wanting to stump the canary, asked what was the square root of 28,561? The bird chirped confidently to 169.

In the morning, I was impressed: not with the canary, but with my subconscious mind, for knowing the math.

Dad is in his office, already at work, and he's taken a loaf of bread into the room with him. But instead of fully closed, the door remains ajar, filling me with the smallest measure of hope.

I look in the fridge. Inside there is a jar of guava jelly and a hard, wizened piece of ginger. In the very back of the pantry, there's a box of linguine, a box of hardened brown sugar, and a bag of almonds, two years past its sell-by date.

I type into the search engine How long to starve to death? and am somewhat heartened by the answer, which is anywhere from three weeks to seventy days. I eat what's left in the jelly jar.

. . .

I head to the high school track where I used to run laps, half-expecting—hoping—to find a wandering canary. It isn't there, of course. There aren't any yellow birds, or any birds at all. But there is my ex–gym teacher, on the ground, searching for something. She says she's looking for a dropped earring.

She looks the same, only grayer. She wears her hair like usual: cropped haircut, miniature pigtails. Her brow is furrowed. She doesn't seem to recognize me. I get on all fours to join her, but the track is very big, and the earring is very lost. The girls' track team descends the bleachers in tiny shorts and ponytails.

"It's green," she tells them. "It's jade."

They drop to the sand. It's a good twenty minutes before one of the girls finds it and holds it up. It's no bigger than a popcorn kernel.

I run six laps, a mile and a half. The high school girls run like beautiful ostriches past me. I am panting by lap number two.

"What's the problem?" my ex–gym teacher says. I am hunched over, catching my breath, wishing I'd eaten something. "What's the problem?" she says again, and I straighten. I jog away from her, without saying anything.

"Hey!" she calls after me. She really was the worst. "Hey, I'm talking to you!"

But I keep running and don't bother to look back.

. . .

On my way home I stop at the grocery store and buy a head of garlic and a can of tomatoes. Canned goods are forbidden, of course, but I am feeling defiant, and how is Mom going to find out, anyway?

Mom's thrown out everything but a glass baking dish. She claims she's shopping for safer cookware. I spread the tomatoes on the baking dish, with salt and oil, brown sugar, slices of garlic, and ancient dried oregano from a sticky plastic shaker.

While the tomatoes are roasting, I rinse the tomato can out and boil the water in the can itself. I cook the pasta in batches in the small can. I toast the almonds from the pantry and blend them with the garlic and the tomatoes and the herbs. Suddenly there is pasta and there is sauce and the semblance of a real meal. I set the table for two. I head upstairs and knock on his door and call "Dad?"

Nothing. I think, *Please, Dad, please, please.* And still nothing.

I'm turning around, unsurprised but still disappointed, when against all odds the study door opens. Against all odds he follows me down the stairs and takes a seat at the set table. Dad eats the pasta, and at first I am too stunned to join him. I can hardly believe my luck.

He asks me how class is, from my perspective. I tell him I think the students are enjoying it, and I am, too. I'm learning a lot. This news pleases him. He washes our two dishes and two forks, pats me on the shoulder, and returns upstairs.

What on earth just happened! I am ecstatic, until it occurs to me that Mom might find the tomato can in the trash. I dig the can out of the trash, put it in a plastic bag, take it to the park, and drop it into a bin there, like it's a bag of dog shit. But even during this excursion, I'm jolly.

This is how calibrated my happiness has become to him: I'm happy all night.

February 11

I consider getting the mail. I decide against getting the mail.

I have all these postal service–related fears, like the fear of mailing letters on Saturday, because I'm worried they'll be lost on the off day. But more relevantly: the fear of running into the mailman while I'm at the mailbox—catching the mailman at the exact time he's filling the mailbox, and having to wait awkwardly.

The fears are unfounded, I know. My mailman in San Francisco was an upstanding guy. Once he tackled somebody who stole a woman's sunglasses from off her face. The thief ran four blocks. The mailman leapt on him and was able to return the sunglasses, intact.

I watch some videos on the Internet that demonstrate how to cook without using pots and pans. For example by putting eggs into a fire.

Another video explains that you can use a basket with water in it, and heat up river rocks, and drop them in, the Native American way. I click on more videos: How to make a candle from an orange. How to open a can without a can opener (but you need a parking lot). A prank that is basically loosening the lid on a ketchup bottle so the ketchup spills all over your pran-kee's food.

It was daytime when I began looking into this, and now, somehow, it's not.

Here's the thing: I cannot eat any more pizza.

What I've been learning from the Alzheimer's forum is that consuming cruciferous vegetables can help with memory loss.

"Cauliflower, cabbage, cress, broccoli, and bok choy," I read aloud to Mom.

"I know, Ruth," she says.

"Eating three servings a day—two hundred grams or seven ounces—can have a significant impact in lowering the risk of dementia and cognitive decline. The research on fruits was not conclusive."

"Cruciferous?"

"That's what it says. Also, walnuts. Berries, all kinds, and folic acid."

"That's interesting," Mom says, not looking up from her magazine.

"I don't object to you cooking," she says, finally. "But I'm taking a little break, myself."

I order new pots and pans online: a stainless-steel collection.

February 14

I'm at Walgreen's to pick up my dad's prescription and laundry detergent when I realize it's Valentine's Day. It's six o'clock. A man holding a briefcase stands in the aisle where the heart-shaped boxes of chocolate are, reading labels. Another man is in the card aisle. Another man twirls all the false roses one by one, indecisively.

Every time I buy detergent I think about the oceans filling with soap and all the fish dying. I know it's not accurate, but isn't it true that all the water we have here on Earth is all the water we are ever going to have?

For dinner I make lamb chops seasoned with rosemary. I read that it's the "herb of remembrance," so I put it on the lamb and I put it in the mashed potatoes. But it's too much rosemary, and it's really not good. What I will remember, I realize, is this failure.

February 16

The chemistry teacher is on week two of his vacation, so we'll meet in last week's classroom.

I suggest tennis before class with a foolproof provocation: "I bet I can whoop you," I say.

"You bet wrong," Dad says, on cue.

And of course he can—he used to do push-ups with me on

his back—but this is not the point. The point is that the car is safe, in a spot where Levin won't be looking. I'm *desperate* to win, though.

"Rematch," I say, for the fourth or fifth time.

He beats me swiftly again and again.

As we're approaching the car, in the parking lot, I can see a little rectangle of paper. A ticket. I whisk it off, hoping to do it fast enough that Dad won't notice, but he does.

"What's that?" he asks.

"Menu," I say.

February 19

Today you asked where babies came from, and I told you that they came from the mall. Where in the mall? you asked, and I told you the Burlington Coat Factory. I told you they were very expensive. I told you they were more expensive than the most expensive coat. We made a game of trying to find the most expensive coat.

I remember the look my mother gave him. It was a look that said, *Are you sure this is a good idea?*

"She won't remember this, Annie," he said, and I thought: *Remember this. You'll show them.*

February 20

Today Dad revives the topic of Joel. He knows that Joel isn't my fiancé anymore, except when he doesn't.

The last trip Joel and I took together was to the beach. He was obsessed with the weather. He'd looked up the UV rating. It was unusually high and bound to give us very bad sunburns so long as we kept not discussing what needed discussing: all that had gone stagnant between us.

We'd driven to Half Moon Bay, for a picnic. We were eating sandwiches, in silence. I like to think each of us was acting out of consideration for the other: knowing we lacked the satisfactory answers, choosing to spare each other the trouble by not asking the questions.

Over by the water, there was a single black braid about to be pulled in, of great interest to the gulls. What I can't figure out is if this thing is specific to me: with some frequency, I'll find artificial hair in public. Instead of coins, it's hair that appears—mainly on sidewalks and streets—improbably often. Together with Joel, there on this beach, was this not uncommon dreadlock.

"Dread," I said, and pointed.

In a week it was over. All our years—that was the end of them.

There was one last thing, I guess: a pelican staggering like a drunk, circling a baby who was laughing in the sand. You know in Japanese, Joel said, the word for beak, *kuchibashi*, means "mouth chopsticks."

Those are more like "mouth ladles," aren't they? was what I said. Later, while he was asleep in the car and I was driving home, I couldn't stop crying.

I'm over it, swear to God. But sometimes a thing washes up, out of nowhere—like an ancient candlestick from some wrecked ship.

Like that time I had appendicitis and, after the operation, was lying miserably in bed. Joel pulled out a deck of hotel cards to pass the time. We played Go Fish. We played Hearts. He held my hand in one of his and with the other started to build a house from the cards. He laid the foundation on my stomach, and I tried my best not to breathe. I tried to hold very still, so I wouldn't be the one to bring it down.

"When you know you've found the one," my father is saying now, "you know you've found the one." About Joel, whom he's forgotten broke my stupid heart.

"But listen, Dad," I have to say.

We met in college. I was standing outside the classroom building, waiting for my next class. I was eating a sandwich, turning slowly like a stand fan, trying to find the wind so it could blow the hair from my face and away from the sandwich. It was peanut butter and jelly and there was the risk of my hair getting caught in the jelly.

"Are you lost?" Joel had asked, justifiably. He invited me to a party that night. I said I'd think about it. In the end, I went only because I flipped this dime: heads meant go and tails meant stay. It had landed heads, so I went, but not before drinking a jelly jar of whiskey in my dorm room. That dime misled me.

The next time I saw Joel after the breakup, it was by accident—a couple of months later. It was Sunday, and we were both at the market on Market. We both had in our hands clear bags of carrots. I was seeing a mechanic named Franklin, who had a weakness for carrot cake and a two-year-old son named Davy. This was week number two of Franklin: we'd last a month.

There was a single tomato in a baggy in Joel's other hand.

"For a salad," he said.

And because we had nothing else to say to each other, I said, of all things, "I've heard some dogs enjoy the odd carrot."

"I didn't know that," he said, and then—to fill the silence—he said, "Someone told me cats can't eat onions. They die if they do."

"You're Ruth," said a woman. "Pleased to meet you."

Joel introduced her as Kristin.

I said something that was supposed to be normal but came out weird: "A pleasure," maybe, or, "Pleasure's all mine."

I already knew about her. I knew about her car with its Oregon plates, parked there outside Joel's and my old apartment, first thing in the morning. I didn't want to see it there, I told myself, but the truth was that I *did* want to see the car, or else why would I have felt that it was necessary to walk down that particular street, past that particular apartment that had been ours, every chance I had, but especially in the mornings, before work? It had to be that something inside me wanted to confirm that it would be there. It always was.

Davy cried when I said goodbye—as though he knew the finality in it—and that was the hardest part, about Franklin. What makes it okay, though, is that there's no way he remembers me now.

You know what else is unfair, about Joel? That I loosened the jar lid, so somebody else could open him.

February 23

"UP! UP! UP!" says the woman in this exercise tape, about our buttocks. As it turns out, Mom's old workout clothes fit me, so I have on her leggings and her tank top and same-size sports bra. And hot pink terry wristbands. I'd unearthed our VCR from the attic to watch them. Mom used these tapes to get back into shape after I was born, which makes me feel I don't know how. She was twenty-five, in her prime childbearing years.

I don't know how I got to be thirty. I don't *feel* thirty, the way I felt so definitely nine, and thirteen, and twenty-one.

This woman has us run, run, run in place. Then she has us do a series of impossible things with our arms.

Now I clean the toilet FASTER, FASTER, FASTER! and flip the pancakes STRONGER, STRONGER, STRONGER!

"Why are you shouting?" Mom asks.

February 24.

The moon, tonight, looks like a cut zucchini coin. I'm filling up on gas at the cheaper station, when somebody says "Ruth." At a different pump, my old friend Reggie is waving enthusiastically. He's immediately recognizable: he looks exactly the same. In high school, we were in a band together. I sang backup vocals and played the guitar. We would practice in his parents' garage. We called ourselves Bambi Mama and our hit song, meaning the song we played constantly, was "The Best Things in Life." It went: "The best things in life / The best things in life are free / The best things in life are Fritos." We had a good time.

Inside the gas station, Reggie buys an Almond Joy for me and a cup of decaf for himself and we sit together on the curb, near the air and water pumps, each of us catching the other up. He'd moved away and moved back recently. First he lived in New York and then he lived in Miami. For a year and a half now he's been teaching drama at our old high school.

There is an animal in the parking lot with us. It looks like a stray dog, but something about it seems different, seems wrong. The creature doesn't have any of that modesty that dogs have. It doesn't seem tentative. It doesn't seem like it wants us to tell it what to do.

"Coyote," Reggie says. "They're getting bolder because of the drought. They're looking for water."

When Reggie says water, the thing comes right up to us, as if summoned. It looks at Reggie first and then it stares at me.

Over us, the moon is emitting its yellow zucchini light. Reggie reaches into his pocket and pulls out something small and shiny: a whistle. He blows on it, it makes a shrill noise, and that's all it takes. The coyote runs away.

"It works on mountain lions, too," he says.

He offers his hand to help me up. I notice the new tattoos on his arms, and a scar on his jaw that's unfamiliar.

He walks me to my car. He says I can get a whistle of my own at the police department, or at city hall.

"For free?" I ask.

"For free. Like the best things in life," Reggie says, grinning. "Like Fritos."

February 25

At three in the morning, I find Dad in front of the TV, watching Ron Popeil sell a Ronco Showtime rotisserie. Dad pushes the loaf of bread that he's sharing the couch with to the side, and pats the seat beside him. I take it.

We fix ourselves peanut butter sandwiches. He cuts his into rectangles; I go triangles.

I remember I used to command him, "Make me a peanut-butter-and-jelly sandwich!" And my dad would say, "Poof! You're a peanut-butter-and-jelly sandwich."

We watch the rotating chickens, mesmerized.

"We could just set it and forget it," Dad repeats softly.

"For a low, low price," I agree. "Just four easy installments."

"Fetch my credit card," Dad says, and we call the 1-800 number to order it.

February 26

I'm getting re-used to these things. The trash trucks. The eucalyptus smell. The quiet and cold mornings during which, unlike in San Francisco, you hardly ever hear any sirens. On a walk this morning I notice a lacquered chopstick in the gutter, its twin down the road. A waitress outside the diner with the $1.99 eggs and sausage, shaking the ashes of her cigarette into a Big Gulp cup. A kid jumping over a line of traffic cones. A bunch of Great Danes being walked that move like horses.

In the park, a woman says SIT to her thin dog. The dog squats but never lets its rear end touch the ground. The woman says SIT to her other dog, and it does the same. That's just how they were raised, I guess.

"Why doesn't somebody get the *mail?*" Mom says, dramatically carrying in an armful of envelopes.

February 27

Grooms, over the phone, is telling me that she has been reading Kevin *Paradise Lost.* Except that, being a baby, he hasn't seemed very interested. Finally she put Scotch tape on his forehead and it was obvious that he preferred the tape.

"Don't be too hard on him," I'm advising. "Remember he's a baby."

At the store, there are potatoes in a bin with this big sign above them that says FRESHLY DUG. They're the size of feet.

Above the avocadoes it says TOUCH ME TENDER.

A woman is stroking a portobello.

"Wow!" she says to me, a complete stranger. "Would you look at the gills on that mushroom!" It endears her to me completely.

Also, while I'm staring at the oils, an alert employee informs me that canola oil is made from rapeseeds! Do I need any help?

At home there are two boxes on the doorstep: two boxes. One is full of loofahs: twelve colorful mesh poufs. Why, we don't know. Dad claims all the pinks.

The other is our Ronco rotisserie that we've forgotten we bought.

I drive back to the store to fetch a chicken. Back at home, we put it in the machine. We set it, but we don't forget it. We watch the chicken turn over and over and over.

"You should definitely buy one," I call Bonnie to tell, breathy with excitement.

February 28

Is this a thing? Lately I'm more forgiving. I used to be very quick to judge the old men who don't know that when you walk past them on the sidewalk where they're sweeping leaves, they should stop sweeping. But now it occurs to me that maybe these old men have maladies—diseases that affect their manners—and should be pardoned.

March 1

I have a dream I'm King Midas but instead of gold it's aluminum. Everything I touch turns to it. I hug my father and *poof!* he turns into a tin man.

"I have a heart," he says sorrowfully. "That's not the problem."

"What's the problem?" I ask, peering at him. He has rust-rimmed eyes.

"I am always cold," he says.

March 2

We're moving class off campus starting this week because Levin's schedule has become erratic, and we no longer feel confident in our ability to avoid him. Theo has spotted him on campus every day this week. Rumor has it that he's having trouble at home, and that's why he's spending all this extra time on campus.

The idea Theo and I plant into Dad's head is that because we're learning about the Los Angeles Aqueduct, we should take an educational field trip to go *visit* it. We should see it in person!

The aqueduct was started in 1908. It would divert water from farms in Owens Valley, whose water was runoff from the Sierra Nevadas. The question was always: Who should get the water, Owens Valley or Los Angeles? Teddy Roosevelt voted in favor of Los Angeles. The farmers were unhappy with that decision. You can still make out the parts of the aqueduct that the farmers dynamited.

Dad is lecturing happily despite the sun, which is beating down on us. Nobody looks comfortable. Sweat is collecting between my boobs and I want to scoop it out.

"That looks heavy," Theo whispers, about my purse.

"It is," I whisper back.

Wordlessly he lifts it off my shoulder and puts it onto his.

March 4

I see, walking on the other side of the street today, a man with enormous pecs. They look as inflated as popcorn bags right after microwaving.

The phrase "born humans" is what I think of whenever I see someone wildly different from me.

Fetal circulation is different from that of born humans.

Fetuses have fine hair all over them that born humans don't have. Fetuses do a thing like breathing that isn't actually breathing—the motions develop their lungs. They take their first breath when they're born and that's when the whole system changes incredibly: unborn to born.

We're *born humans*, I think, about the huge-pec'ed man. With our functioning circulatory systems. Breathing, walking, having real hair. Just *look* at us.

Later, at the farmers' market, I watch a couple bros sample dates.

"Shit," says one bro, coughing. "I think I'm allergic to this giant raisin!"

"That's not a raisin, Steve," says another bro. "That's a Medjool date."

Born humans, I remind myself.

March 5

We're at Home Depot because Dad's decided he wants to finish building the covering for the patio. He abandoned the project years ago, when I was in high school. In a book called *Backyard Structures*, we find a photo of the thing he wants to build: a "pergola," the book says, and provides a list of materials and steps, like a recipe. We load a cart with fresh two-by-fours and buy a new saw blade to replace his rusted one. Near the cash registers, an old woman is struggling to pull some orange buckets apart. Dad helps her.

We tie red bandannas to the wood that juts from the car's open trunk and cross our fingers that the cops don't pull us over.

My grandfather was a carpenter and a roofer.

"But I'm afraid of heights," is what Dad confesses to me now.

March 6

Today you asked if I'd ever watched a moth eat clothes and I replied honestly: no.

Today you said you didn't believe it!

Today you admired a magnolia tree and I told you that it was one of the earth's oldest plants, that the flowers are so big because beetles used to crawl into them carrying the pollen on their legs. And you asked, Why should I believe you? And that was a very good question.

March 7

Linus called, so I'm trying to chop a bell pepper one-handed, and making slow progress. He's telling me about his latest argument with Rita, which was over what to have for dinner. *I don't care*, she said, when it was clear, he said, that she did.

This week Rita got back from Bali, where she'd been for a month, doing yoga and drinking fruit juice. As of three days ago, she's back, looking fitter than she ever has, and now they are being awkward with each other. Linus worries that he has gained as much weight as she's lost. They are having trouble getting back into the swing of things.

"You'd think we'd have so much to talk about. In terms of, like, ground to cover. Stuff that happened while we were apart," he says. "But when I ask her questions, it's like she's hesitating—deciding what to tell me. Or she'll answer in a really bare-bones way."

"It's not that easy, to *say what happened*," I say. "What happened to you, for example, yesterday?"

"I tried to talk to my girlfriend about her vacation, that's what happened."

There's a pause.

"What if she met someone?" he says.

"You're overthinking this," I say. I try to sound convincing, reassuring.

"Let's talk about something else," he says.

I tell him about what I read today: that scientists have learned how to embed false memories in mice. Using pulses of light, they were able to make the mice remember something that never happened: something unpleasant. The mice showed fear, remembering the thing that happened that had never *actually* happened.

Memories are stored in collections of cells, and when we remember, we reassemble the cells like a puzzle.

A few years ago, they figured out how to give mice déjà vus. They gave the mice the feeling of having been somewhere before.

Last year they figured out how to implant memories in a piece of brain in a test tube. Which—whatever, is my feeling. Why don't they figure out how to keep mice from forgetting things? We don't need *more* memories. It's hard enough trying to get a handle on the ones we've got.

"What do you think happens to all the mice?" I ask Linus.

"I hope they're retired somewhere," Linus says.

"I hope someone is feeding them gouda and giving them massages."

"And they're fat. And they're happy."

"Is that Linus?" Mom asks, peeking into the kitchen, and I nod. "Let me talk to him," she says, taking my phone.

"Hi, dear," I hear her say.

March 9

Theo has sent me a photo of his parking permit and I've been on the computer, trying to counterfeit one for the car. The font isn't exactly right, but it's close enough, I figure. Not close enough to use in the actual parking lot, but realistic enough to appease Dad. I glue-stick the faux permit to the front windshield.

Today we're in a lecture hall because Harry, one of Dad's students, tipped us off that his philosophy teacher, who typically teaches a class on Plato during our exact time slot, has been out with the flu. The space is comically large—big enough to accommodate 150 students. The eight of us settle into the first two rows.

Today he's talking about the gold rush, which those of us who grew up in California already know something about from our fifth-grade curriculums: the tens of thousands of men who came in hopes of striking it rich.

We panned for planted gold at Knott's Berry Farm. In the books we read, men had to bathe in champagne because water was too expensive, and women sold pear blossoms to prospectors—tagging the trees with their names. One day they'd become pears or they wouldn't. Everything was a gamble back then. Everything maybe still is.

Every day in San Francisco, on my commute home, I would pass the same elderly Asian woman, standing on a street corner, holding a napkin to her face and giggling behind it, playing peekaboo with nobody. Once a man talking to a mail slot turned to me and told me he was an angel. All I had on me was a five-dollar bill, which I gave to him.

A long time ago I stopped wondering why there were so many crazy people. What surprises me now is that there are so many sane ones.

After class, Theo and I convene at his apartment, to do what teaching assistants are supposed to do. What we've told Dad is that we're entering essay grades into the computer system. But actually we're eating delivery pad Thai and reading the notes

Dad's written on students' papers. The notes are critical but thoughtful; the papers are long and well researched and earnest. I'm choking up a little bit at this whole unbelievable situation.

"How was your bedside manner, working at the hospital?" Theo asks.

"Unobtrusive," I say. "Like a lamp."

After I tell him about the loofahs, he shakes his head.

"Sometimes it's just the way of the universe," he says. "Once I got a ten-pound box of sour belts."

"Did you send it back?"

"Not going to dignify that with a response," he says.

Now he's squinting at his fortune.

"Are you," I ask, "*farsighted?*"

Immediately he looks sheepish.

I read it out loud for him: "You will grow slightly fatter every year."

He fishes his glasses from his backpack.

Joel had better vision than I did, and so he was the one who, in the mornings, when we woke up, could tell me the time.

Sometimes I think: he could see things coming that I couldn't.

The last ultrasound I gave was to a woman named Lucille. She was five months pregnant with a boy. I said something only marginally funny and she peed all over the examination table.

That they're called "pregnancy symptoms" has always struck me as strange—*symptoms*, I mean. I remember the start of a yoga class, the instructor asking if anybody had any injuries, and a pregnant woman raising her hand.

"Well, you know." She shrugged.

Same thing with "patient." At the hospital the other day, the doctor, referring to Dad, called him "the Alzheimer's patient." Patient for *what*, I wanted to ask.

"Earth to Ruth," Theo says. "You okay?"

Later at home my phone rings and it's Grooms, who, instead of saying hello, is weeping into the phone. Kevin said "blah"! The most chill first word.

March 10

Dad's in the backyard, cutting up wood and cursing. I'm walking to the library to return the DVD when a small child on a scooter shrieks at me: "A WOMAN!" In case, I guess, I'd forgotten.

Lately my thing is inventing new yoga poses. The Onion is one. You make yourself very round, then peel yourself, limb by limb.

March 11

Tonight I try my hand at dessert: baked Alaska, because of course. It's so epic! How can you bake *Alaska*? How can you *not*?

March 12

I'm losing it, too. I intended to return a book to the library but dropped it, by mistake, into a mailbox. At the library, where I've gone to explain myself, I run into Regina, who was homecoming queen our junior year. She had hay-colored hair to her waist and I envied it. She has children now. They share names with hurricanes—I don't know if it is intentional or what.

"This is Katrina and this is Sandy," she introduces. The children are four and eight, and even so young, their expressions look overcast.

March 13

Okay, and then today: I dropped stamped mail into a trash can.

Online I read that the youngest person to have ever been diagnosed with Alzheimer's was aged thirty.

March 14

I'm spending the weekend with Bonnie. We are at the drive-through. Someday we'll make more money, Bonnie is certain. I'm less. For now we're buying hamburgers because cheese is ninety-nine cents more. Bonnie has slices stowed away in a pocket in her purse that we insert into our burgers.

After, at an estate sale, inside a tackle box, we find a compartment with teeth in it: filled and gold-capped teeth, and bits of pried-out gold fillings. We buy them.

We have a job to do tonight: we're seat-filling for the Oscars—there to make the ceremony look full. Bonnie talked her boss into letting me work, too. We're sharing the same tube of Chanel. The color is "Pirate." I'm wearing loaned diamonds, and Brad Pitt is two rows away.

In the bathroom, we discuss things I could do for an actual living. I could get a job nannying? Parents I did ultrasounds for would sometimes bring me their born babies—let me hold them.

"No," Bonnie remarks, without missing a beat. "Repeat what you just said to yourself."

Afterward, we're paid in cash, and we decide to spend it at Jared's sushi restaurant. The restaurant is called Tomorrow. It's in a strip mall in Tujunga, and we have to step over a dead cat in the parking lot.

We order *omakaze*. Seeing us, Jared claps his hands together. He carves me a rose from a radish.

"Let's see that eel peeling," I say, and he turns suddenly shy.

It's fine. The sushi is fine. Because there's no alcohol at home, I haven't had a drink in weeks. I put too much sake into my body, by mistake.

Back at Bonnie's place, I say to Bonnie, "Let me cut your hair, just to try."

"This is terrible," she says, once I'm through, staring into her reflection. "That's my professional opinion."

March 16

The sun is out and it feels like spring so we propose having class outside, which Dad thinks is a great idea. He suggests the lawn outside the library; we suggest Mission San Gabriel for the historical element. It's not chronological, Dad protests. We're past the 1700s. But we have our way, and the class divides into carpools. We spend the sunny day in the grass, all of us in sunglasses, in view of the tombstones.

On the way home Theo, Dad, and I, in Theo's Subaru, stop by an In-N-Out. Theo orders a hamburger rather than a cheeseburger. I hold the burger hostage instead of immediately handing it over, and interrogate.

"Why a hamburger? Because it's cheaper?"

"It's not that," he says. "It's just, I don't know if it's worth it. I don't think I can taste the cheese."

March 18

Mom and Dad are watching a recording of this year's Oscars, to see if Bonnie and I are visible. All the actresses in ball gowns tell us what they're wearing: *I'm wearing Dior Haute Couture. I'm wearing one hundred small emeralds. I just had a cheeseburger, I'm starving.*

And Dad pokes fun at the actors and actresses—remembers all their names, like any regular, not sick person.

It's Mom who finds us. She pushes pause and points her finger to the screen, and there we are, though out of focus: Bonnie and me in our borrowed dresses and jewels and too-bright lipstick, looking not like ourselves.

"Brad Pitt!" Mom exclaims, thrilled. "Look how close you are!"

March 20

Because I've read that sulforaphane, produced in the body, and found in broccoli, can help keep the brain sharp, I cook broccoli for lunch and broccoli for dinner.

The vegetables are called "cruciferous" because their flowers are cross-shaped, I also read.

Sometimes I switch it up with cauliflower. I cook small, oily fish for their omega-3s. For breakfast we have oatmeal with flaxseeds, which also have omega-3s, and berries, which have antioxidants.

A diet can't *reverse* harm that's already done, I know. But what if it could halt the decline?

I'm looking for stamps. If I send in these empty coffee bags I'll get a five-dollar manufacturer's rebate. Five dollars buys me another bag of beans. The goal is to keep this up forever and never buy coffee again.

My stamp search is turning up empty. What I find in the junk drawer, instead, are divorce papers, with signatures from both my parents, dated the year before last—meaning well *after* the physicist was purportedly out of the picture.

I remember my parents used to let me have their old check-books, and the fake checks I used to write—to Linus, to my parents—worth billions. "VOID," I would write on the memo line. Maybe, I thought, this had been somebody's idea of an imaginative game. Divorce papers, all filled out.

I can't be in this house because of everything. Plus the kitchen sink is spitting food up and there's a wasps' nest the size of a head outside underneath the awning. I head to the Laundromat with our hampers. It's a reassuring thought, that the machines work there.

Outside the Laundromat, two drunks are sharing a cigarette. The man has a hand tenderly cradling the back of the woman's head, which she appears to enjoy at first, before she begins to resent it.

"You think it's lumpy," she says, pulling away, suddenly. "You think my head is lumpy."

"I don't think it's lumpy," he says.

"You do," she says. "You think it's lumpy."

"Baby, I love your head," he says.

"You're saying I'm not smart," she says. "Is that what you're incinerating?"

He says, "I'm not incinerating a thing."

"It's nothing," my mother says, when I ask about the papers. We're watching a show on TV: families are having their homes redecorated by TV show people, who insist the families throw out all their belongings with sentimental value and replace them with brand-new items. The people always protest when their things are thrown out.

"Mom," I say.

"Shhhhhhh," she says, while a video game console gets appraised.

"No way in hail," says the owner of the video game console, unwilling to let it go.

There was a time, I'm now remembering: she let Linus cry, until my dad finally came home and changed his dirty diaper.

What could that have meant? That was before everything went wrong, though, wasn't it?

March 22

Now I'm just looking in every drawer, like it's my job.

Cleaning the guest room, I find, in a drawer, written in my mother's hand, on the back of an unopened envelope:

Howard:

— Leaving empty bottles in the car's center console.

— Crashing into a shrub in front of the house.

— Peeling open a bunch of bananas, one by one, and abandoning them naked on the table.

— Saying to me, Here's a thought: I do not deserve you.

And below:

Howard drunk; Howard causing me sadness.

Howard, Howard, Howard.

In the glove compartment of his car I find expired packets of mustard. They were once my dad's, I know, to fool my mother and the Breathalyzer.

Also in the glove compartment: a photo from the first family vacation I can remember, a trip to Washington, DC. On the subway, coming back from the Lincoln Memorial, Linus and I were in a pair of seats, and my mom and dad in seats opposite each other. Leaving the memorial, they'd just gotten into an argument—who knows what the subject was.

On the train, my dad had patted the seat next to him, a way to beckon her over. She shook her head slowly and seriously and tried to keep a stern face. It had taken a moment before she smiled.

Later, in the house, I find a photo of us, at the actual memorial: Linus is bright pink, like he's been crying, and my parents are scowling and I'm eyeing the man with the cart full of ice cream, in the corner.

"Let's not talk about this now, okay?" Mom says.

She rubs lotion into her hands and then opens the newspaper.

"For better grip," she says, from behind it.

"You can ask me anything, dear," she adds. "Just . . . later."

I wonder if this is why my mother asked me to stay: she didn't want to be alone with him.

"Don't blame anyone else," was what William Mulholland said, we learned, when the St. Francis Dam failed. "You just fasten it on me. If there was an error in human judgment, I was the human."

Fasten a failure! Like a pin on a necktie.

March 23

Class this week is off campus. Because it's raining and there's a leak, Theo tells Dad. We're crowded around a small table at a café. A cupping is happening: they've given us little cups of beans that we are to smell.

Joan, a graduate student, maybe my age, always sits near Dad. She has far-apart eyes and long, blond hair. Actually, none of her hair isn't impressive. Her eyelashes curve in this logic-defying way, as if each set of lashes might be able to support a mothball or a marble. She bears a resemblance to Kristin, Joel's new girl-friend. They look like they might own the same breed of dog or buy the same type of groceries. Immediately I don't like her.

I notice Joan trying to catch his eye, my dad not picking up on it. That's when I realize, *Oh*, and try not to follow that thought any further.

"Why her?" I'd asked Joel, about Kristin.

I don't know why I thought he'd give me an answer.

Outside, there are undergraduates putting tags on trees.

When I ask what's going on, one of the girls says, "We're tracking squirrels." That's the moment Theo appears beside me.

"Squirrel teeth, I recently learned," he says, "grow *continuously*. It's something like six inches every year. But eating all those nuts and things keeps their teeth from ever getting that long."

"I don't believe you," I say. Dad and Joan are talking. They aren't touching. But for some reason, beneath the doorway, they look like two people who've slept together.

"Believe me or don't: it's true," Theo is saying.

"So if we trapped a squirrel, and tied its hands and feet behind its back—"

"And fed it."

"And fed it. A strict no-nut diet."

"Or a liquid nut diet—"

"Liquid nut?"

"Like almond milk. Or peanut butter."

"A liquid nut diet of almond milk and peanut butter—"

"We could grow a saber-tooth squirrel." Theo nods.

I try not to make it obvious that I am watching Joan, who is talking with my father, who is shaking his head.

"How cool would that be?"

"What?" I say.

"The squirrel," he says.

"Very," I agree.

I watch Howard put a hand on Joan's shoulder, to say goodbye.

"You're not as into this as I am," he says.

"The squirrel?" I say.

He nods.

"It sounds dangerous," I say. "That's all."

I look over and Joan is gone and my father is alone, and when he sees me he taps his watch.

March 24

Okay, but listen: this is why I so seldom visited. I didn't want Linus's claims confirmed. I wanted to preserve my memory of my perfect father. I didn't want to know the many ways he'd hurt my mother. I didn't want to have to pick sides. Unlike my brother, I wouldn't have been able to do it as easily.

A couple of years ago, Dad visited me in San Francisco. He was in town for an academic conference, and staying at a hotel downtown. We had an early dinner with Joel, but Joel was on call, so he left Dad and me to drink together.

At first it was exciting: I had never seen him drink to excess; I had never gotten drunk with my dad before. It felt like a way to be closer. But then it became apparent we weren't drinking *together*: he was drinking like it was a race. And I drank and drank to keep up.

I don't know how many drinks in we were when he confessed to having had that affair with the physics professor, the one that Linus had told me about, and that I had hoped to myself wasn't true. It was years ago, he continued, and it had been a mistake. He loved my mother. He felt that he was still being punished, even though it had happened so long ago. He didn't know how to make things right, but he would—he had to.

Did he bring up divorce then?

Try as hard as I can to remember, I can't.

I don't remember making the decision to go to bed. I woke up on the hotel couch, jeans still on, a blanket pulled over me. On the floor was an empty bottle of whiskey, drained, and another bottle of wine I don't remember.

Dad left for the airport early, and I could smell whiskey on him when we hugged goodbye.

It was clear he didn't remember much of the night. He didn't seem ashamed about it. I was still a little drunk. Everything smelled like alcohol and was repulsive. The smell might have been coming from inside my nose. I could smell it in the waistband of my jeans, so I took them off and chucked them across the room. I picked up a glass of water that was sitting on the nightstand, took a swig, and spat it out: it was gin or vodka or some combination of the two. I tidied the hotel room in my underwear—throwing the bottles away, straightening things. I drew myself a bath.

"What happened?" Joel said when he picked me up. My hair was still wet from the bath; my face was pink. I burst into tears, hideously. I hiccupped the whole drive home.

March 26

Mom's been heading straight to the living room after work. Today she takes a bag of popcorn and a plate of the broccoli I've made for dinner—"Good," she nods—and turns on the TV. I join her. The star of the show is a bachelor who is to select his future wife from a group of women. He is an ex–soccer star. He calls all the women "*gills.*" "There are so many beautiful gills to choose from," he says. "How is it possible I can ever be able to make this choice?"

During commercial breaks it's:

- Mom changing the subject.
- Mom balancing popcorn on my knee.
- Mom not letting me in on things and me having trouble eliciting it from her.

And Dad without a clue. Eating his dinner, screwing pieces of wood to other pieces of wood, cautiously climbing a ladder, oblivious to any atmospheric disturbance.

• • •

I walk to the nearest bus stop and board the bus. I get on with-out looking to see which bus it is. Not that I know what any of the numbers mean.

A couple is sitting on the bus. The young woman is feeding her boyfriend yogurt.

A mouth, if you aren't interested in the person it belongs to, is disgusting.

The couple gets off the bus, and a large man in a police uni-form gets on. I wonder what happened to his car.

"Hey, stranger," somebody else says to him. His face snaps out of his dull bus-riding face.

"Hey," he says. "Hey."

"How many kids you got now?" she asks.

"Five," he says.

Before I know it, we're at the last stop. I don't know what city we're in. There are warehouses all around me—a vast, unending parking lot.

I try Reggie—my only friend still in town—but he doesn't pick up. I dial PHILLIP, and Theo answers after the first ring.

"This is embarrassing," I say, "but could you give me a ride home?"

"Where are you?" he says.

"I'm sorry," I say, and read him the cross streets.

He picks me up after not too long and doesn't ask what hap-pened, which I appreciate. Instead he tells me about his day.

How he was, when I called, leaving a bad stand-up show and feeling outrage. How, earlier today, he returned bad avocadoes to the grocery store, and got a refund, and felt triumphant.

We've been in the car for an hour. He pulls into my driveway.

"Can we, I don't know, sit here for a second?" I ask.

"Sure," he says, still not asking any questions, and which I still appreciate.

"What happened with them?" I finally ask Theo. Theo who knows Dad, who knows Joan.

He inhales, holds his breath for a second.

"It's really none of my business," he says. "There was a flirtation between them. Text messages. I think it started last semester, lasted a couple months. She said he led her on. He didn't seem to think so." He pauses. "It's over, I think. Whatever it was."

"But," I say. "Did anything happen?"

"No!" Theo responds, sounding surprised. "I mean, I didn't even . . . I don't know. I doubt it. I don't think so."

He looks, concerned, at me. He touches my shoulder.

"You're gonna be okay?"

"I think so," I say, opening the car door. "Thanks for getting me."

"Anytime," he says.

"Anytime?"

"Well, at least a few more times." He smiles. "Maybe, like, four more times?"

"A gentleman," I say, and turn toward our house. I turn back around before I enter and see he's still looking. He gives a small wave and drives off.

Class today is at a Chinese restaurant called the Golden Lotus. On topic because Dad's lesson is about the Chinese in California: by 1880, Chinese from Canton were a tenth of California's population—first because of the gold rush, and then as workers on a railroad that would link the West Coast with the East. The Chinese men—and they were nearly all men—labored steadily and well. They could work longer hours than white men, who were nevertheless dicks to them.

There's an early bird dinner special. We sit around the lazy Susan and spin fried rice and broccoli beef. I'm not in the mood.

There's Joan, again, next to Dad, always flashing her white teeth, always pouring him tea, and using chopsticks in a stupid way, with her hand held absurdly high on the sticks.

The soap won't lather and the reason, it turns out, is Dad's painted the bar with clear nail polish. "April fool's," he says, happily.

April 2

I ask Dad how he and Mom met. Of course I've heard it before; I just want to hear it again. She'd appeared the first day of class, and he'd been drawn to her immediately. They'd gone to a student art opening together. They'd stolen a bottle of wine from the gallery—concealed in a purse—and escaped to the park to drink it.

This is when it occurs to me that it isn't the story of my mother he's telling—that actually, it's the story of how he met someone else. He's telling me about Joan.

"And didn't you go to a Mexican restaurant after that?" I try to prompt.

"It was Ethiopian." He frowns.

"Didn't you eat tortilla chips?" I'm persisting.

"That can't be right," he says, with this expression, as though he's hurt that I don't trust his details.

My mother had also been his student, but that was different. They were both graduate students. After the semester was over, he asked her to have a drink. They went to a happy hour at a Mexican restaurant, where the deal was cheap drinks and all-you-can-eat tortilla chips. They shared a pitcher of sangria, and when a song with maracas came on my mother said she loved salsa. My father panicked a little, unsure if now was the appropriate time to admit he couldn't dance. When he raised a chip to his mouth, my mother produced a homemade jar of it, triumphantly, from her purse. My father ate, relieved.

. . .

My parents had their wedding in Palm Springs, and my uncle
John, ordained for the day, married them.

"May you love each other till the cows come home," John
said. "May all your quarrels be water off a duck's back."

He called me the other day—John did—in a panic.

"I locked my keys in the car," he said. "I'm losing it, Ruth."

"Did you call triple A?"

"It's unlocked now."

"You're fine."

"I'm a goner."

I was about to ask him what he knew about the divorce,
when I changed my mind, unsure of how I'd put it—unready,
also, to find out. Instead I asked him about my mom's parents,
who died when she was six months pregnant with me. She
had been their only child. Sometimes the loss still seemed so
powerful I hesitated to ask her anything, and she rarely volun-
teered.

"Polite Arizonans," he said, "who cut a mean rug. They
danced all night at the wedding. They were wacky. It's probably
where you get it from."

We're not really related though, I don't say.

"She was too young," John said.

There was a pause so long I thought we'd been disconnected.

"Hello?" I said.

"Your mom, though," John said. "She doesn't take any shit.
It was all about you, after that."

April 3

Dad leaves the door to the study open, which I take to mean I am welcome to enter. Inside there's an aquarium: a big tank with water in it, and a water pump going, and little blue rocks at the bottom, plastic seaweeds waving gently.

"No fish, Dad?" I say.

"I knew it was missing something," he says.

We go to the pet store. We watch the fish for a while. There are depressed-looking sea snails, sucking algae slowly. It occurs to me that they might be taking their time, *enjoying* the algae. Maybe they aren't depressed after all. Maybe it's the opposite, and the one who's depressed is me.

There is a crowded tank of transparent guppies. There is a lonely angelfish. We watch an employee shake fish flakes into the water, and I like the sound the tube of food makes. But Dad doesn't seem interested, particularly, in any of the fish or snails.

We stop by the reptile tanks and watch an iguana chewing a collard green. The turtles are being fed their crickets and there is a cricket that escapes. "Escape" maybe isn't the word. It jumps neatly into the iguana tank.

"Shit," the employee says, as the iguana eats the wayward cricket. "He's an herbivore. He's supposed to be an herbivore!"

This guy, the pet store employee whose job it is to feed the turtles their crickets, has to be about my age. He's been telling us that iguanas shouldn't eat iceberg lettuce because iceberg lettuce has no nutritional value, and an issue is that iguanas can get addicted to it, refusing to eat anything else.

• • •

My father hasn't picked any fish or turtles or snails. He seems displeased with the store's selection. I don't want to waste the trip, so I pick up a bag of birdseed, a specialty mix with sunflower and thistle seeds, and millet. In the section with the seeds, an employee named Bill wants to sell me a "wildlife block," a fifteen-pound cube of seeds.

"Attractive to birds, yes," Bill says. "But also a variety of critters!"

"I'm not sure," I say. It seems excessive.

At the very last minute Dad picks out six miniature scuba divers: diverse divers, plastic men of every hair and skin type. At home, into the tank they go.

April 4

We've been seeing more of John, who has been stopping by once or twice a week now. He's been dating a woman he met on the Internet. Her name is Lisa, and she lives in Rancho Cucamonga. She works at the animal shelter. When he visits, I give him a shot of cabbage juice.

Today, while Dad is at the gym with his brother, I let myself into his office again. I open his desk drawers and rifle through them, expecting to find I don't know what: some proof or clue or sign.

I know it's pointless. I know it's stupid and impossible. I

know significance, more often than not, is invisible, imbued on things like saltshakers Joel and I stole from the overpriced French restaurant, or the toy from the vending machine, or some sad thing we found on the street and saved.

In the drawers there are packets of instant oatmeal. There are business cards and restaurant matchbooks and a little glass panda bear and a stress ball shaped like a brain. For all I know the oatmeal might be a gift from Joan or the physics professor, and the panda and brain had been gifts from Joan or the physics professor, and the matchbooks are from restaurants of some significance to them. But because there is no way of knowing, and because the scuba divers in the fish tank are watching me judgmentally, I stop looking.

April 5

There's a page on his desk I read guiltily:

> *Today, when I told you to behave, you roared angrily: I'M BEING HAVE.*
>
> *Today, after I took my socks off, you touched my ankles—the impressions that had been left.*
>
> *Today you put my hand on the impression left by your sock. My hand could circle your whole miniature ankle.*
>
> *Today, after you lost a tooth, you cried that you looked like a pumpkin.*

> *Today I had to stop by the post office, and you looked around and said, aghast, "This is errands?"*
> *Today, while I was changing your brother's diaper, and putting baby powder on him, you burst into tears and begged me not to put too much salt on him.*
> *Today you were so readily impressed by me.*

April 6

Class today is at Señor Amigo's. We're eating chips and fajitas. I situate myself between Dad and Joan.

"We're here," he says, "to learn about the Chinese in California."

He then proceeds to repeat last week's lesson, unbeknownst to himself.

We look around at one another, eyebrows raised.

My heart drops. He was doing well. We don't mention it.

Layla, our teenage waitress, stops by our section to say hello.

"This is my class," Dad says proudly, gesturing at us.

"This is my daughter," Dad introduces me.

"Ruth, right?" she says, smiling pleasantly, then brings us a few more bowls of guacamole.

April 7

I've been packing lunches for Mom and writing jokes on the napkins, like this is going to cheer us both up.

"Why do dinosaurs make bad omelets?" I write on one side of the napkin.

On the other side: "Because their eggs stink!"

I draw a winking face on her orange.

Mom's latest thing is making 3-D paper collages. Home from work, in the time she used to spend cooking dinner, she cuts out pictures with an X-Acto knife and glues them together, carefully tweezing layer upon layer.

April 8

I'm standing in front of a Burger King, waiting for Bonnie, when it starts to rain. Bonnie waves from across the wide street and begins to make her way over, jellyfish-like under her clear umbrella. There's one other person outside the restaurant with me. Her eyeshadow is metallic and reminds me of an Andes mint. Her boots are the soft kind and not meant to be getting wet. She's holding seventy-five percent of a Whopper in one hand and a cell phone in the other, and into it she's arguing about whether or not to keep dating her boyfriend, who sounds like a real deadbeat.

Her burger's getting wet and I whisper to Bonnie that I'm worried about it. Also the shoes. We collect her underneath the umbrella with us. She's still talking into the phone but raises the Whopper in appreciation. We huddle beneath that small, clear umbrella, watching the people inside the Burger King and the drops collecting through Bonnie's clear umbrella. She's telling her friend on the other end of the line that last night he'd told her, *"STAY, BITCH."*

Afterward we ask her if she's going to stay, and she shrugs. "I guess so," she says.

Later, while we're eating burritos at the cantina, Bonnie says, about my parents, "You're not allowed to think about this."

"I have to," I say.

"You don't know anything about it," she says, "on top of which, it's none of your business."

We each dip a chip in silence.

"In other news," Bonnie says, "things are lighting up in my career sector."

"Is this a horoscope thing?" I say.

"And I checked yours," she says. "The stars say: it's not a good time to tackle deep issues; it's a time for pleasant interactions."

April 9

I'm at the store looking for groovy macaroni—macaroni with grooves in it. My mom used to always make this casserole with green bell peppers and ground beef and macaroni. She called it groovy macaroni. Whenever I try to make it, it isn't right. It's always too something.

"Ruth?" says a voice behind me.

My high school friend Deb is standing in the aisle with me, in front of the boxed juices. The last time we saw each other was ten years ago, this time of year. She was the first person I ever met who cared so deeply about her weight she wouldn't eat anything. I met her long before it had occurred to me that somebody might choose to eat nothing. I would later in life meet plenty of people who were the same. She was just memorable to me because she was my first.

Deb wouldn't use ChapStick because she was scared it would make her fat. She wouldn't lick envelopes because of the calories. She wouldn't chew gum. She boasted to me that at communion, her trick was to crumble the body of Christ and drop the crumbs onto the floor until the wafer was completely gone, or almost. The little plastic cup of wine was enough to make her tipsy.

Now we're at the store together. She is wearing a sundress and a straw hat and she's gained a lot of weight. She has a little girl with her, and a baby in the other arm. The girl looks about six and is also chubby.

Was pretending I didn't recognize her the correct thing to do? I turn that over in my mind for a second.

She says hello first.

"You look great," I say. And she *does*. The thinness had always been awkward on her. She shrugs.

"How's William?" I try. William was her high school boyfriend, her baby daddy. What I remember about William was that he had tattoos and wore thin pants better than everybody else; he understood how they looked on him better than other high schoolers did. He seemed mature. Later I learned he'd been held back twice, and maybe that was why he knew better about the pants.

"We split last year." She shrugs again.

"Bella, this is Ruth," Deb says. "Say hi to Ruth."

"Rude," Bella says.

"*Ruth*," Deb says. "Say *Ruth*."

"Rude," Bella says again. I deserve it. She's doing a little dance.

"That means she needs to pee," Deb says. "Could you hold her?"

She hands the baby to me without waiting for my answer and the baby scrunches her face like she's going to break into a loud wail very soon and I jiggle her to keep the wail at bay and rhythmically read her the labels on bottles: Ocean Spray Cran-Apple, Sunsweet Plum Smart, Welch's 100% Grape Juice, Welch's 100% Grape Juice with Calcium.

There's a blooming warmth in the diaper region. *You're taking a massive shit right now, aren't you*, I whisper to this baby, still jiggling her, until her mother—after what seems like an hour—rematerializes to take her back.

I'm feeling a scratch in my throat so I buy a tube of Airborne and a bottle of water. In the supermarket parking lot I unscrew the water and Airborne. But the tablet is too big to fit into the mouth of the bottle. So I hold it in my mouth—this is painful—and let it fizzle until it's small enough to fit through.

This morning I get a Facebook request from Deb. "Nice to run into an old friend ☺."

And now she's forwarding me e-mails at an impressive clip.

One says: "If you are ever thrown into the trunk of a car, kick out the back taillights and stick your arm out the hole and start waving like crazy. The driver won't see you, but everybody else will. This has saved lives."

"How to lose 2000 Calories!!!!" and then a video of a chicken dancing.

Also "THE MOST DANGEROUS CHOCOLATE CAKE IN THE WORLD." I click on this.

"Why, you ask??? Well, from the moment you decide to make it until you sit down to eat is about 5 minutes! So, now chocolate cake is no more than five minutes away at any time!" And then there's a list of ingredients you're supposed to mix in a microwave-proof mug, and nuke.

In an ancient *National Geographic* I find in the bathroom magazine stack, I read that jellyfish synthesize a special protein that helps with dementia. When elderly people are given jellyfish to eat twice a week, they are less likely to develop dementia or other age-related diseases. Another fact: most jellyfish have one opening that serves as both mouth and anus. (Except the box jellyfish: 64 anuses!)

Now I'm calling all the stores. None carry jellyfish.

April 12

I peel myself a hard-boiled egg, but in the unsatisfying way: the shell comes off in small shards but also with large chunks of white attached. I drink coffee. I don't feel like washing the coffeepot. I walk to the living room, where my father is spread out on the length of the couch. Dad moves his feet, one after another, so I can take a seat next to him.

Now and then I'm tempted to shake him.

What were you thinking? I want to scream sometimes, on behalf of my mother. Or, *What is wrong with you?*

One of Dad's socks falls off in the process of moving his feet for me. He shrugs and, using his foot, pulls the other one off, too.

I make us THE MOST DANGEROUS CHOCOLATE CAKE IN THE WORLD. Two dangerous chocolate cakes, each containing three tablespoons of chocolate chips. They look like beautiful soufflés fresh out of the microwave. I e-mail Deb a picture.

There are four more classes for this semester, and then it will be time for final papers. Theo and I are out of ideas for relevant venues. We're out of ideas for irrelevant ones, too. How about class at Disneyland—we'll talk about the role of the entertainment industry in California?—Theo suggests, and Dad complies, happily.

At Disneyland, we meet Mickey and Minnie Mouse. We eat Popsicles. We stand in a lot of lines, and Dad uses them as opportunities to lecture. We get our photo taken on Splash Mountain, looking like the strangest family. On the spinning teacups, Dad is totally gleeful.

"This was a good idea," I whisper to Theo, during the fireworks over the Magic Castle.

"It was Joan's," Theo says quietly back.

Later, at home, a urinal cake falls out of Dad's pocket.

"Why do you have this, Dad?"

"I don't know," he says, troubled.

Going out to get the mail today, I run into the mailman at the mailbox. But it turns out not to be so bad! It's overcast outside, though the actual rain hasn't started, and the mailman is wearing blue shorts and a poncho. He has a white bandage wound around his calf. There is the one normal calf, and the other one, which looks like a snake that had swallowed a soft-ball.

"That dogs hate mailmen," he tells me, "is true."

"Is it bad?" I ask.

"It was a German shepherd." He shrugs. "It could've been worse."

"What's worse than a German shepherd?"

He hands the mail to me. There's a bright Band-Aid on his thumb.

"Was that a dog, too?"

"That was an orange," he says. "That was when I hurt my thumb opening an orange."

April 15

Today there are four goldfish in bags on our countertop. They look unhappy.

"A troubling," Dad tells me. "That's what you call a group of goldfish."

April 16

Bonnie is babysitting in Thousand Oaks and I'm here to help. The children belong to Bonnie's boss at the art gallery, and the babysitting is expected of her; she isn't paid overtime. They are seven and five, and their names are Ralph and Lou Jr.

Their mother is on a date, at the ice-skating rink with a banker. While they are skating, the four of us sit at the elegant dining-room table, eating reheated chicken tetrazzini.

"Chickens are the cousins of the dinosaurs," Ralph informs us.

"Not any dinosaur," Lou Jr. corrects, "the Tyrannosaurus Rex!"

"If dinosaurs still roamed the earth, I'd sic one on Lou," Ralph says.

"That's not very nice," Bonnie says.

"Not *this* Lou," Ralph says. "I just mean my dad."

There is a pause.

"Well, that's not very nice, either," Bonnie says.

After putting the kids to bed, we dismantle a pomegranate from the tree in the yard, careful not to crush the seeds into the carpet. Bonnie shows me, on her phone, photos of what she's been working on lately: full-length cutouts of herself, stretched to different heights, and Photoshopped to different widths, like paper dolls. There are big and small and fat and skinny Bonnies. She's tiny in comparison to the tallest cutout—it's maybe nine feet tall, towering over her.

"Help me with my statement," she says.

"Bonnie Nazaryan is interested in possibility"—I clear my throat, use my art-critic voice—"in the infinity of lives unlived."

"Bonnie Nazaryan," she says, "is terrified of amounting to nothing, terrified of having lived on Earth without leaving a trace—trying to announce to anyone who will listen—her best friend mostly—*I exist!* Pathetic. *Here I am!*"

We browse Ralph and Lou's mother's movie collection. Her ex-husband, Lou Sr., is in the entertainment industry, and very famous.

I see *Eight O'Clock Coffee* and hold it up.

"What's that?"

"My dad's in this," I say.

I've never seen it—it's impossible to find a copy. I've only ever read the script. What I don't remember is that the story begins with *suicide*, the same way I always forget that all Jimmy Stewart wants, for a good part of *It's a Wonderful Life*, is to kill himself.

The premise, in my father's movie, is kind of nutty. It takes place in this woman's afterlife, which looks a lot like an old California ghost town: dirt roads, horse-drawn carriages, saloons with swinging doors. The population, all the dead people, are literally hollow. They have no bones or internal organs. On windy days they have to wear heavy coats or else risk being blown away.

In the movie, the main character—an actress who later played a murder victim on an episode of *Law & Order*—is meeting an old flame of hers. My father is sitting behind them, at the bar, eating an olive from a toothpick. His hair is wavy and he's maybe my age. He looks just like Linus.

"Wow," Bonnie says. "He was smoking hot."

On the way home I stop in Alhambra, at the Chinese grocery store, to look for jellyfish, which they have. I buy six packets of frozen jellyfish and six packets of dried.

I linger to watch an employee gently pressing avocados, adhering "RIPE" stickers to the ripe ones.

April 17

Tonight I prepare a jellyfish feast.

- Jellyfish salad, Thai-style
- Jellyfish soup
- Jellyfish fritters
- Jellyfish pickles

Jellyfish spaghetti, with jellyfish noodles and jellyfish sauce. The eaters are not exactly enthusiastic, but they are, at least, polite.

April 18

Theo is at the door. Through the peephole I can see he is holding a container of yogurt.

"Your dad home?" he asks me.

"He isn't," I say. He's at the gym with John.

Theo opens the yogurt lid. Inside there is what looks like ruffles of a party dress, bright and green and metallic, all bunched up at the bottom of the container.

"It's *Actinodiscus*," he says. "It's a good beginner coral."

"It's beautiful," I say. "Thank you."

"Thank my brother," Theo says. "He grows corals."

"Grows corals?"

"He grows and sells corals. This one is really special. It's priced per polyp."

We put the coral into the tank, where it looks very glamorous.

He takes a book off the shelf and starts flipping through it.

"Hey," I say, "do you want to come to LA?" I'm supposed to see Reggie perform some art.

He says it sounds like fun. He gets in my car and we go. He switches the stations on every commercial but pauses on KOST 103.5. He calls in to try to win tickets to an exclusive acoustic Alanis Morissette show.

"It's ringing!" he says.

They're looking for the fifth caller, but he is the second, and we feel a very specific, bittersweet disappointment.

This is Reggie's performance: he's painted gold, like a Buddha. He peels the wrappers off little banana candies, licks each candy, sticks it to himself. This takes an hour.

Once he's covered in candies and there are no candies remaining in the bag, he begins to dance like a god, and sings sweetly.

Reggie can't really say hi, and we can't really stay for his whole performance, but he *looks* appreciative. I think.

Outside the gallery, in the gutter, there's a ball of black hair.

"I think it's called a *coleta*," Theo says. "I just read about this somewhere. It's a clip-on bun. Matadors wear them."

I'm *always* seeing hair everywhere, I tell Theo, who is unimpressed—doesn't think this is special.

"You could start paying attention to socks, for example," Theo says. "Socks are everywhere. Especially baby socks. Seriously, look." And he points to something baby blue on the sidewalk—a little blue sock for a baby.

April 20

Today is Dad's birthday, so class is at home. Mom's skipped book club; she's here, too.

I've baked a cake. I've bought Dad another goldfish—a fancier one. At the pet store, I picked one with pretty but modest, unshowy fins. In the tank he (or she?) gulps and gulps and gulps.

Theo comes over with a different coral and a birthday card for my dad, and a book for me. He's loaning me a book with the same size spine as the one he borrowed, to patch up the hole in the shelf.

All the male students are flirting with my mom, asking for embarrassing stories about Dad. Joan, I notice, only smiles politely and avoids her. Joan's in some kind of animated conversation with the class's two other women, who don't appear to see that Joan's heart's not really in it.

I can only fit thirty candles on the cake—a chocolate cake with chocolate frosting, and some walnuts on it, for good measure. Thirty lit candles turn out to be rip-roaring enough.

"Happy thirtieth to me," Dad says, and blows out the candles, which are terrifyingly ablaze. He eats a slice and then cuts another.

"I have no memory of eating that last slice of cake," he says, "except that it was delicious."

April 22

Joel calls while I am at the dollar store considering packages of athletic socks, and I let it ring. But who am I kidding? I can only pretend to be interested in the socks for so long. I choose black ones and chuck them into the shopping cart. I check to see if Joel has left a message, and he has.

"Ruth," it says. "I just met a pygmy goat. His name was Noah. Anyway"—Joel pauses—"I don't know why I called. I guess I thought you'd like that. I forgot that their pupils are kind of square."

At home, trying the socks on, I see that they have ON THE GO! printed, in pink, on the toes.

And though I try really, really hard not to, later, alone, I re-listen to Joel's message about the goat.

Their pupils are kind of square!

I guess I thought you'd like that.

April 25

"Could this be true?" I've called Grooms, and I'm asking. "Every day, we lose one hundred thousand brain cells." I've read this in the *Los Angeles Times*.

"Yes," she says. "True."

April 27

In 1860 and 1861, before the telegram, the Pony Express was the fastest means of communication between the East Coast and West. There used to be celebrity mailmen! Of course the actual Pony Express went over the Sierra Nevadas, and not to Southern California. *But wouldn't it be educational to have class on horseback?* we suggest to Dad. He agrees happily.

On horseback, Dad attempts to shout educational details about the Pony Express. It's difficult to hear him over the *clickety-clack*.

There's a couple, also on horseback, in front of us, saunter-ing. The horse in front of us is speckled. Some shit falls out of its butt and we avoid it. The man turns his head. My heart falls straight down. It's Levin.

"Howard," Levin says, then looks at me, then Theo, then Joan, and the rest of the students. "What's this?" he says.

"We're learning about the Pony Express," Dad explains, sheepishly. "A little unconventionally," he says, with a laugh.

"What do you mean?" Levin says, evenly.

"It's so nice to run into you!" I interject, panicking.

"My California history class," my father says.

"What California history class?" Levin says. My dad looks at Levin, then back at me. And suddenly he understands.

"How do we stop these things?" Dad asks, gruffly. His horse jerks forward.

His horse stands and sways. Dad looks all around him, for the exit.

Theo dismounts. "Move your hands up his neck and lean forward," he says. "Swing your right leg around, and slide down." All of us watch as Theo reaches up to help.

"Now slide down," he says. "I'll spot you."

Theo puts both hands on Dad's waist. Dad slides off clumsily. He almost falls backward, but Theo catches him.

"Howard," Theo says, holding our horses' reins. "We can explain."

"Let's go, Ruth," he says, avoiding everyone's penitent gaze, in the tone he used to use when I was in high school, having done something that displeased him.

He says nothing during the car ride home, and nothing afterward once we're at home. He only makes a pot of coffee, and takes the entire pot into his office.

April 28

We hadn't planned for this.

Everyone calls; everyone writes.

We meant well!

We love you!

And on and on.

Dad has shut himself in his office. He won't answer Theo's phone calls.

I slide him tortillas. He writes LEAVE ME ALONE on one in ballpoint pen and pushes it back out the door.

May 1

Still nothing from Dad. Theo comes by, and we camp together outside the door.

"I'm sorry, Howard," Theo shouts at the door. "We shouldn't have lied."

We stay camped outside the office for hours. We play a few games of chess.

Finally a note emerges from underneath the door: ABOUT TO PEE IN JAR. PLEASE GO AWAY.

We consider staying. We leave.

May 2

I haven't seen a single bird enjoying the food mix, but somehow, the seed supply in the feeder is diminishing. All this time, I've been wondering how it was possible, but now I'm watching: a squirrel, indulging. And still Dad won't speak to me.

May 3

Today, we notice a tall stack of frames Dad's put outside his office door. His teaching awards.

Mom collects them, puts them away. "We'll put them back up when he feels better," she says.

May 4

Dad's emerged from the office but is still not a fan of me. He speaks only with my mother, and in a dramatic whisper, so I can't hear.

To me, he doesn't say more than a few words—the occasional question. "Where's the coffee?" That sort of thing.

The fish are getting fatter. The fish, in fact, are obese.

Today I see why: I watch Dad feed the fish, sit down, and, minutes later, rise to feed them again.

I remember reading that there was a time Auguste was eating cauliflower and pork, and Alzheimer asked her what she was eating, and she said, "Spinach."

That's something like what happened today, which was that today I made pork chops and potatoes, and Dad said, "I don't want this," and I said, "This is exactly what you asked for," because it was exactly what he had asked for, I'd even gone out to the store to get the pork and the potatoes specifically because he'd asked for them, and then I had looked up a recipe for pork chops and the best way to do them. I'd put them in a brine and cooked them with apples and balsamic vinegar.

"I don't want tomatoes," he said.

"There aren't any tomatoes in there," I said. I said it very calmly.

What happened next was that he shouted at me. He shouted that he wasn't a child and he knew what tomatoes were and those were tomatoes, and that he was my father, and what was my problem, that I couldn't show him some respect. My first instinct was to put the steak knife away because I had never seen him like this, and because I was frightened. I put it in my back pocket. He saw what I had done with the knife, seemed insulted that I thought he might be dangerous, and took his plate and threw it against the wall. It shattered, on cue.

I gathered the rest of the steak knives from the silverware drawer, hurried out of the house, and threw the knives away, still shaking. I took everything out to the curb. When I got back inside, Dad had retreated upstairs.

I swept up the plate pieces. The sweeping was calming and after I felt calm enough I made a plate for myself. I ate the potatoes with a soup spoon and a pork chop with one hand, as if it were a slice of pizza, in front of the television. *Oprah* was on but I kept the volume off, reading the closed captioning from time to time but mostly not. The show was about the secrets to long life and I just wasn't in the mood. Everyone had his or her own secrets. For a 105-year-old secretary and housekeeper, it was not having sex. There was a man who swore by cold showers. I picked loose strands from the couch. I wondered: If I sat there all day, picking, would the couch unravel into nothing?

Suddenly Linus, like a mind reader, calls.

"I'm coming home," Linus says, over the telephone. The spring semester is over; he's working on his dissertation.

"I bought a ticket," he says.

I want to ask why he's *buying* tickets, if something had happened between him and Rita and she didn't finagle him a free one, but I don't.

May 13

At the airport, a woman holds her breasts with her hand as she races from the ticket counter to her departure gate. Someone tries to sell me flowers. I think about buying some mums for Linus, but then I spot my tall brother, a head or two above everyone else, green duffel slung over a shoulder.

And because a sandwich is the only thing anybody ever wants after a plane ride, even a short trip like Linus's, we don't drive straight home. We stop in downtown LA to get sandwiches at our favorite deli. We sit in a booth across from each other, with Linus's duffel at our feet because he's paranoid about leaving luggage in the car.

A man sitting a booth to our right might be John Travolta. He is with another man who is short, bald, and fat, but in a compact, somewhat attractive way. They are both eating salads.

Linus and I stare at the laminated menu even though we already know what we're going to order. I want a Reuben with everything and the bread buttered on both sides. I want coleslaw. First we want to share a dish of pickled herring. Our order is so obvious to us, we almost forget to tell our waitress.

"How is he?" Linus says.

"Well," I say. "He's not so thrilled with me."

Earlier in the day he had forgotten the word for pencil. He called a mechanical pencil a *needle*. Then we passed some evergreens and he called the needles *pens*.

The fat man is saying to John Travolta that his wife has been intractable, ever since their dog lingered by her breast.

"She heard that schnauzers can smell cancer," the fat man says.

"I wouldn't put it past them," remarks John Travolta. He signals to the waitress and asks for a slice of cheesecake.

"You, too?" he asks the fat man.

"I'm going to weigh three hundred pounds," the fat man chuckles, "but okay."

I tell Linus about yesterday. Our father took too many fish oil capsules by mistake. First he threw up, then he had a nosebleed, and we used the entirety of a roll of paper towels to get all the vomit and blood. He was embarrassed. He made me promise not to tell my mother. I promised I wouldn't, and after dinner, when she asked if anything exciting had happened, I didn't let on that anything had.

Now he is at the door, awaiting our arrival.

"Hi, Dad," Linus says, sounding wary.

"Son," Dad says. He takes Linus's bag with one hand and embraces him with his free arm, first trying to reach over Linus's shoulder, ultimately wrapping the arm around Linus's waist, on account of the height difference. We go inside and drink coffee Dad has brewed, like regular people with nothing the matter. At first, anyway.

When Dad asks how Rita is, Linus says he thinks she's good.

"I mean, I think," he adds.

"Things 'weren't really working' for her," Linus says, without intonation.

"I'm sorry," our father says, really looking it. He touches Linus on the shoulder, and Linus flinches a little.

"It's fine, Dad." Linus downs his coffee and picks up the duffel. "It's whatever."

Later, when Mom gets home, I notice the two of them on the couch, talking quietly. The TV is on but they're not watching. Mom is saying something, a hand on his arm. Linus's head is hanging, listening. Because Dad is bellowing something at me from upstairs, I almost miss it.

May 15

We've done it before, obviously, but now we're unsure how to inhabit this house together—Dad, Linus, and me. In the living room, Dad asks Linus about his studies and receives terse responses. In the kitchen, Linus occasionally says, "I can help you with that," when he notices Dad reaching for something in a cabinet or bending over to get something.

"It's a late birthday present." Linus hands Dad a small wrapped package.

It's a crossword puzzle book.

"Keep me sharp?" Dad laughs.

Linus bristles. "If you don't want it, I'll take it," he says, hurt. "I don't care."

"Hang on," I say, running upstairs to get my pencil with the orange eraser. I hand it to Dad. "For the crosswords," I say.

May 18

Joan is on the phone, and she's saying, "Would it be okay if I spoke to your father?" To me!

"I don't know if that's a good idea," I say.

"I understand," she says. "But—"

"Look, I'm his *daughter*," I say.

"He doesn't remember me," she says quietly.

"What doesn't he remember?" I say, and Joan gets very quiet.

"It's the short-term memory," Lung had said, that's the first to go.

May 19

Now she has the nerve to give me a note for him. She's left it in the mailbox, addressed to me, but inside my envelope there's a sealed envelope for him.

Which of course I throw away.

May 21

Today Mom announces that some students of my father's are coming over and hands me a grocery list. When I get home, Joan is there and so is Theo and they're arranging crackers on a platter.

"Ruth!" Joan says, and hugs me.

I pull out the Brie—misshapen because it was bagged, unwisely, at the bottom—and Theo helps to reshape it.

Who invited her? and *Why is this happening?* are questions I am dying to ask him, but I don't have a chance to. He seems grateful to be in my father's company—eager to be forgiven.

Dinner is take-out Thai. The curries have been transferred to bowls, the papaya salad to a platter, and there are place mats and forks and knives and napkins: Joan sits across from Linus, who has no idea who she is besides a student, or what she means; I'm across from Theo; my parents are at the table ends.

Dinner proceeds as though Joan and Theo are a girlfriend and boyfriend Linus and I have brought home from college and introduced. My parents ask about their upbringings. My parents tell them stories about Linus and me as kids, for their benefit. Joan and Theo laugh appropriately, because *how cute those people were*, who were us and who are not us, and now they know about the time Linus and I were in the bathtub together, and a piece of poo floated to the surface, and each of us pointed to the other, and to this day they haven't gotten a straight answer about who's to blame. We'll never tell. I'm watching my father, to see where he's looking, but it's normal. He's not paying any particular attention to her; he's looking at whoever's doing the talking. Meanwhile, I can feel Theo's eyes on me. I can't bring myself to meet them.

They leave together. After Linus hastily loads the dishwasher and retreats upstairs—to watch TV on his laptop, we can hear it—Dad retires for the night, and it is finally just my mother and I who remain in the kitchen, wordlessly drying the dishes. She's drying a large white platter, making circles on its surface with a white dishrag. Holding the platter, she looks so small. When she says something finally, it's to call Joan *lovely*, as in, "She was lovely."

"Damn it, Mom," I say, unable to help it—the anger that's rising.

"Damn what, Ruth?" she says, quietly, and already I regret what I've said—what I'm about to say.

"What," I say, "are you trying to accomplish here?"

She puts the platter down. It seems as though she might smash it, but instead she takes a glass from the table and begins polishing that.

"I don't appreciate that tone, Ruth," she says, very calmly, the way she always used to say it.

"She doesn't mean anything to him anymore," I say.

"And what," she says very flatly, "could you know?"

"I know you don't deserve this shit," I say. "Things are over between her and Dad. Whatever the things were. None of this is your fault."

Mom doesn't respond. She looks only a little ruffled, as though someone has unexpectedly handed her a warm water balloon.

"He doesn't. Even. Remember," I say.

She says nothing. I know this means: *But I do.*

She ignores my question. What she says, instead, is: "You have no right."

And it shouldn't surprise me—this asserting of herself—but it does.

"Why couldn't you visit, Ruth?" she asks, quietly. "Why couldn't you manage to visit?"

This, I don't know how to answer.

Truthfully? *I didn't want to see you suffering. I didn't want my fears confirmed. It was less terrifying this way: not helping you, not saving you, just leaving you all alone.*

And then quietly, she adds, "This wasn't how I thought it would be."

"It?" I say.

"Having a daughter," she says.

She removes her gloves and hands them to me, all without saying a word. "It's fine," she says, quietly, leaving me to finish the dishes.

May 22

Today, home from work, she skips dinner and retreats to the master bedroom. She's put a comforter on the couch in the study, for my father. No pillow, so I give him one from my bed. He seems genuinely confused.

May 23

She leaves the house for work and gets home after dinner.

I ask where she's been and she says only, "Swimming," and locks the bedroom door behind her.

Night three and my dad bangs on the door and shouts, "ANNIE, I LOVE YOU," like it's a dorm building, and he's nineteen and declaring his affection dramatically. But it doesn't open.

We think maybe she's crawled out the window.

It's always this: someone on one side of a door, someone on the other.

I remember one late night in college, I was in the dining commons, bracing myself for the long night of studying ahead, putting a tea bag in the mug of hot water to steep. Outside it was snowing, which was a marvel for that first year of college—having just moved from California—and tedious for the other two and a half. I was watching the snow.

Linus had called, upset, because my father wasn't coming home, and my mother was being her usual self, too patient and too forgiving, and Linus thought she was being unreasonable—being unreasonably patient—and Linus really, truly wanted to do something about it, but he didn't know what he could do, and neither did I.

"It's like she thinks she deserves it," Linus had said, "or something."

"That makes no sense," I'd said. Outside, kids I recognized from my dorm were patting snow into giant men: snow people engaged in erotic acts.

It doesn't matter who remembers what, I guess, so long as somebody remembers something.

May 28

Today you asked me what "Dick" meant, and while
I was deciding what direction I should take, you
said, "Mom said you were one."

Today you put on your mother's earrings inside
your ears, and we had to shake them out.

Today you asked me, "What are nerds?" And
when I said, "They're people who are smart, and
really interested in studying a subject," you said
that your mother had told you there were no nerds
in your elbow, and that's why it didn't hurt when
you pinched there. Nerves! I thought, but didn't
correct you.

I rip up the page. I mean to throw the pieces away but can't. I put the pieces into my pocket to throw away later, or to forget to take out of my pocket and have destroyed by the washing machine.

It's all so messed up. I think what it is, is that when I was young, my mother was her best version of herself. And here I am, now, a shitty grown-up, and messing it all up, and a disappointment.

What imperfect carriers of love we are, and what imperfect givers. That the reasons we can care for one another can have nothing to do with the person cared for. That it has only to do with who *we* were around that person—what we felt about that person.

Here's the fear: she gave to us, and we took from her, until she disappeared.

May 29

At four this morning, there is loud knocking at the door, and someone shouting, "POLICE!" From the top of the stairs I see my mother and Linus, squinting at the cops—there was a woman, a man—shining their flashlights and asking if this is Howard Young's house. Mom says it is.

"He was two streets over, sitting on a porch," they say. "We got a phone call. The neighbors were worried." And there is Dad, behind them, in only boxers.

"Well, it looks like your clothes are here," says the man cop. The pants and shirt are spread across the couch—they look as though they've been laid there. The cop reaches into his pants pocket. "Seems like your wallet is here, too."

Dad looks stunned. He sits down. Mom thanks the police, and when they are gone, she sits beside my father, who starts to cry. Still wordlessly she wraps her arms around him, kisses him on the side of his face, and repeats, very softly, "Stupid, stupid, stupid," and kisses him some more. This is how we leave them.

Sometimes what I wonder is if it counts, I hope, for anything. All that time with Joel, I mean. There was the day, for example, we went fishing, and used chicken nuggets as bait. What I remember is the day itself—brisk with a breeze—and what the sun looked like, and how we laughed. In the end, we threw back all the mullet we caught.

"Christ, these fish eat *chicken*," was what I had said.

"Christ, these fish eat *nuggets*," Joel said.

Then he ushered me into Tommy's, where we drank pitcher after pitcher of sangria until the sugar became too much to bear.

That was a good night. But here I'm conceding it wasn't anything.

What I want to know is what counted for something and what counted not at all. Now I feel like a shit for spending that time—that's the word it's convention to use: *spending*—on what turns out not to matter, and neglecting the things that did, and do.

After Joel and after Franklin, there was, very briefly, a painter named Adam who used to say, "Bore goo," and it took me a long time to realize he meant *bourgeois*. But I forgave it, because who am I to judge? For a long time I thought *touché* meant *touchy*, and also that *homely* meant *resembling home*.

After the breakup, which was nasty, an envelope came in the mail, from Adam. There was no note, only a piece of string. I couldn't figure it out. I kept it laid out on my desk until I realized what it was: string cut to the length of the circumference of his penis.

David, the attorney, took me on three dates—each of them to steak houses. Always, it seemed, he would eat and drink less than I did. It caused me this private anguish. The second date, at a different steak house, over another top sirloin, he said, "I'd like to do this again," and as he said it, I knew that I didn't.

Patrick was a policeman. He was mild and kind and he looked all right.

Late one night, at somebody's housewarming party, he turned to me and held my right hand in both of his, as though he had something important to say.

"What is it?" I said.

"I was thinking," he said. He wasn't very bright, and really looked like he had been.

"You know the rescue dogs, after 9/11?" he said. "The ones who would look for survivors in the rubble? Something I heard, the other day, is that, during the searches, they would grow depressed, going long stretches of time without finding anybody. The relief workers would take turns hiding in the rubble so the dogs could find them and have the strength to carry on."

"You're calling me a dog? That's what you're doing?" I said, drinking my beer, which was by now warm. I had been struggling to identify the taste while Patrick was talking and now I realized what it was: tortillas. This beer tasted like tortillas. Listening to Patrick, I'd been hoping—against hope, that much was clear—he had something to say that could change my mind.

"No, what I'm saying is, I could be the relief worker," Patrick said. "I could surprise you. It could give you strength to go on."

"Look, I'm sorry, Patrick," I said. "It just doesn't work," I said, "if you *tell* me how it's supposed to go."

There was a pause then.

"I'm sorry, too," was what he said, finally.

The other day, talking with Bonnie, I said something about Joel. Something reminded me of Joel and I mentioned it, offhandedly. We fell into a silence.

"If I were you, I'd forget about Joel," she said.

"I didn't mean anything."

"I know you didn't. I'm just saying, if I were you, I'd forget about him."

If I were you is something I've never really understood. Why say, "If I were you"? Why say, "If I were you," when the problem is you're *not* me? I wish people would say, "Since I am me," followed by whatever advice it is they have.

I have always felt bad about the year of friendship that Bonnie and I lost: the year I left college to be with Joel in Connecticut, Bonnie and I fell out of touch. She kept asking if being with him—leaving college to do that—was a good idea and I, not wanting to entertain the possibility that it might not be, stopped returning her calls.

When I finally answered one, two months later, she didn't bother to pussyfoot.

"This is a dumb idea," she said. "You're not thinking this through."

"You went to art school," I said, meaning: *That doesn't even count as college.*

"I'm trying to help," she said before hanging up, "and you're being a bitch."

She's since told me that, that year we didn't speak, she had an Afro.

What a thing to have missed.

On the Alzheimer's message board, I introduce myself and write:

> I don't know if I'm cut out for this.
>
> This job is for someone purer of heart.

And the responses come:

> No one here has never not thought that.
>
> Your heart is in the right place. Or close enough.
>
> Your heart has nothing to do with this.
>
> You know what the origin of that phrase is, "cut out"? It's from tailors. Having their cloth cut out for them.

Things that take up room in my brain that I wish didn't:

- 3.14159265
- The names of all the world's major and minor straits
- The entire screenplay of *Mrs. Doubtfire*

- How to turn an unwritable VHS tape into a writable one (tape over the little square in the lower right-hand corner)
- "We Didn't Start the Fire"
- Ditto "Gangsta's Paradise"
- The catalog of movies Joel has seen, at least up until last year
- Parakeet diseases
- Various taxonomic ranks
- The knowledge that the king of hearts, in a deck of cards, has no mustache, while the kings of spades, clubs, and diamonds do

Dad's study is a mess. It's my fault, for not checking it out sooner. The smell, when I open the door, is awful. There are half-eaten sandwiches in the drawers, and there's mold on the bread. It looks like Dad has ripped pages from books and is assembling the disparate pages. There's one stack of pages he's rebound with craft glue and construction paper, as though he's building a better book, compiling a book of separate books, a book that would improve upon the originals.

There is a bedsheet draped over the fish tank, and who knows how long it's been there. The fish are still swimming, but their bodies seem drained of gold. They're small ghost fish.

I call the pet store, and it's Bill who answers. He says not to worry: goldfish cells produce pigment in response to light. Leave a goldfish in the dark, he says, and in time it will turn completely white.

Downstairs, my father has peeled a clementine, and now he's sitting at the table, looking at this skin that's fallen from the fruit in the shape of two perfect lungs.

Here, now, I'm wishing things were different. The other day I read that patients in later stages of the disease will eat the entire banana or orange. They will fail to recognize the peel.

It's a terminal disease, all the literature keeps saying.

"But isn't everything terminal?" is what I say to nobody, out loud.

June 1

And then, somehow, it gets better.

Dad, Linus, and I go for morning walks, and on our walks we notice bicyclists having a good time. We tell ourselves we'll dust our bikes off and bike around ourselves, and another day we follow through: we ride our bikes past the community pool, and vow to bring our swimsuits back for a swim, which we do. We stop at the grocery store for cruciferous vegetables. Linus borrows DVDs from the library—movies we've never heard of, and mostly they're bad, but still.

June 2

We're at the store looking for capers and can't find them.

"Can I help you?" the employee asks.

"We're looking for capers," Dad says.

"That's a kind of fish, right?"

"It's like a tiny olive," I say.

Somehow she leads us straight to them.

June 3

I've bookmarked a recipe I want to try: *patati con agnello scappato*, potatoes with escaped lamb. There is no lamb. From now on I'm going to make macaroni and cheese "with escaped beef" and rice pilaf "with escaped pig."

Linus is in the guest room, supposedly writing. I can hear Dad singing in the bathroom, revising Smokey Robinson: *Though she might be cute, she's just a prostitute, you're my permanent one.*

Mom joins me in the kitchen, not saying anything. She picks up a peeler and starts to peel potatoes. It's her first time in the kitchen in who knows how long. I'm too surprised to comment. Out the window, our new neighbors Rollerblade by, the woman in her sports bra, the man wearing knee pads, obviously mad at each other but unwilling to neglect their exercise regimen—skating angrily.

From across the kitchen, Mom tosses a peeled potato into the stockpot. I try and miss; it lands in the carafe of coffee, splashing coffee everywhere. Mom shoots another one perfectly into the stockpot. Mine flies out the window. Mom laughs and laughs.

"There's a potato in my coffee," Linus remarks later.

"Potato?" Mom and I say innocently, at the exact same time. We crack right back up.

June 5

Mom isn't in the mood for driving so I drive her to the doctor's office for her regular physical. I nearly hit a stopped car, looking at the reflection of her pretty, just graying hair in the windshield. This is a fact: my mother is beautiful. When she was nineteen she broke her back and, after it healed, got a tattoo over the damaged vertebra. As a teenager, she chipped her front tooth on a jam seed. Her eyes have always made me think of pitted olives, the way they remind you—in case you've forgotten—that pupils are empty.

In the waiting room, under the fluorescent light, her transparent, vein-rich wrist, holding a water bottle, looks even more transparent. I never once heard my dad say she looked pretty. Instead he'd say, "Annie, you look so memorable."

During the worst of it, my father was regularly carrying gin to class in a clear plastic water bottle. There was a day my mother found him passed out on the couch, with his shoes and tie still on, sleep talking as though to a classroom.

When my mother noticed him, she took off his shoes, removed his tie like a wife who might greet her husband home from work. Then she unbuttoned his shirt and gently lifted him out of his pants and boxer shorts, and left him to sleep in the nude in the living room until morning. She is telling me, now, that why she did this—out of kindness or malice—she still isn't positive.

"You know what I miss the most?" I remember her telling me once, on a vacation to Mexico we took together in my sophomore year of college, after we'd had a couple of margaritas. "I miss that time your dad broke his leg."

He'd fallen from the apex of an A-frame ladder. He'd ascended in the first place to extract leaves lodged in the basketball net. That was a long time ago: I was fourteen. After the injury they would practice walking backward. It was doctor's orders, because going backward puts less strain on the knees. Mom would hold both Dad's arms as he proceeded slowly in reverse—even up and down the stairs. He needed her, and that's what she missed.

"Of course he needs you," I'd said. I still don't know if it was true back then. In any case, it was becoming true now. It was what my mother had wanted, although these circumstances were different, perhaps, from what we had pictured.

In a tabloid in the waiting room I read that Blake Lively's mother, lacking blush, once licked an Advil and rubbed its pink on her cheeks.

Dr. Lung talks differently to my mother than he does to my father. When my mother asks him how he's doing, he tells her. He tells her that they went on a vacation—he and Mrs. Lung, without the kids—to the Bahamas.

"You see this?" he says happily, removing his glasses, showing her the white stripes of skin on his temples and nose, hidden behind the band—evidence of his tan.

Nearing the end of the appointment, Lung says that caregivers will often ask him what they can do.

There's nothing really to "do," he says. Just be present.

"Like in the moment?" I say.

"I meant 'around,'" he says. "But sure, that, too."

June 6

The present: there's this woman in the same aisle of the supermarket, curling a large dog bone like it's a barbell.

June 7

The present: glancing in the mirror, I notice a segment of noodle on my cheek. But I can't remember the last time I ate noodles.

June 8

The present: we pound schnitzel with Dad's dictionary that we've plastic-wrapped.

June 11

The present: he doesn't mention Joan. He doesn't mention the physicist.

June 12

The present: he's saying everything with a Southern twang and making Mom laugh and laugh.

The present: Mom laughs so hard she loudly farts.

June 13

The present: Linus and I are lifting Bonnie's couch from the moving truck to her new living room. Vince, Bonnie explains, is shooting a commercial for Audi.

The present: on the freeway, on the drive back, I notice a black truck that says EAT MORE ENDIVE on the side.

The present: I scream, "That's Carl!"

The present: "Drive, drive, drive!" I command Linus.

But when he pulls up beside the truck it isn't Carl after all. This trucker is fatter and paler.

"Who's Carl?" Linus asks.

"He drives endives," I say, so disappointed.

June 14

The present: I wash the windows and clear, from the sill, what seems like a hundred perished ladybugs.

June 15

The present: Linus cooks us French toast for dinner and we're out of syrup, so we go to the door of a new neighbor and inquire. She has a little Aunt Jemima.

June 16

The present: a little boy, walking between his parents, screams, "I don't like dogs!" when a pair of joggers jogs by with their Chihuahuas.

His mother leans down to whisper something—maybe tell him that's not appropriate? In response, he clarifies, very loudly, "I don't like SMALL dogs."

                                                        June 22

The present: I chip out a tile in the bathroom. I start to pull on the caulk, and it comes out in one long strip, like it's the tub's hangnail.

                                                        June 23

The present: the carpet cleaners are here. We push all the furniture—the coffee table and ottomans and armchairs—to the tiled kitchen. The shampoo takes the morning, and afterward, we open the windows and sliding glass doors to rid the room of the chemical smell.

The present: I go to the store to buy milk and when I get home, there is my dad, perched on top of the coffee table, head between his knees in the crash position: like he's on a plane about to make an emergency landing.

June 25

The present: Mom's asleep and it's just the two of us, past midnight, watching TV, and Dad says, "You're my daughter?"

"I'm your daughter," I say.

"You sound different," he says.

"How?" I say.

"More sonorous," is what he says.

"Well, thank you," is what I say.

June 29

The present: the phone rings and it's Theo asking do I want to get breakfast tomorrow?

June 30

The present: we're eating eggs. He's telling me about visiting his older sister, and her toilet paper roll holder that plays "Ring of Fire" when you unspool the toilet paper. Why "Ring of Fire," he's asking, and not something more relevant?

"A Boy Named Poo," he says.

"Pee of heartbreak?" I try.

"Exactly," he says.

• • •

Now he's lifting bacon and asking, "So you and Joel—that was your longest relationship?"

I tell him about the time, after the breakup, when I was sitting in the park having a picnic alone, a pigeon flew overhead and shat into my Tupperware of macaroni. How I considered simply scooping the shit out and continuing my meal.

How my friend Sam, who drives a refrigerated truck—he delivers produce and meat to restaurants in the Marina—was the one who helped me move to that new apartment. We unloaded it all together, and at the end, Sam patted me respectfully on the back, like I was an old, dying dog, and wished me luck, and I laughed, like, of course it was all under control. Sam liked Joel and me equally, or so it seemed, then—he hadn't chosen sides.

How that first night, everything was cold: the couch was cold, the lamps were cold to switch on, my bed too big and too cold and my body couldn't make enough heat to fill it.

How I'd swat at moths and reprimand myself. "You're so mean!" I once said, loudly, to me.

And then it became pronouncing foreign labels out loud: *yerba maté*, I caught myself saying, really rolling the *R. Jalapeño*, I read the can. Like a crazy, broken-up-with person.

How, one of those first nights, walking home to what should have been our new apartment, it was after midnight, and I'd had a few drinks. Two point five, like Grooms advised. Not too many. And there was a hunched-over man with an eye stitched shut and a mouth of glinting gold teeth sitting on a stoop, and when I tried to walk fast, past him, without making eye contact, he said, "Be safe."

"Thank you," it took me a moment to say.

The present: I'm saying, "Your turn."

She was his college girlfriend. They met in their junior year of college, on the Ultimate Frisbee team. She whupped him good. She had a beautiful voice. Has, I mean.

"Was she your longest?" I ask.

"Not the longest," he says. "But the most severe."

They broke up because things didn't feel right, according to her. But two weeks after the breakup she was cavorting openly with a photographer, who took her pictures and posted them on the Internet. Theo would have dreams set exclusively in dark rooms—everybody whispering, and glowing red.

This is what he's telling me *now*, in the present. I'm not cheating here.

The present: Theo reading from Dad's textbook in a Katharine Hepburn voice.

The present: me saying, but why did everyone talk like that, back then? Like Katharine Hepburn?

The present: Theo dipping a chocolate-covered cookie into his tea and it dissolving immediately, and his panic.

The present: me laughing uncontrollably.

The present: me remembering, *Don't get me wrong.* It was what Joel had said. But I did! I got it all wrong.

And: *be present*, and the words falling behind me, quickly, into the past, too.

July 1

Sugar ants have crawled into the space beneath my laptop keys. This happened after I ate a Popsicle over my computer. They've taken up residence and now they won't leave. For a week they've been my tiny advisers.

I'll type, "What color blouse," and wait for an ant to come up. If it crawls out from "R" that means "Red" and if it crawls out from "P" that means "Purple," and if it is a yes or no question, I'll wait for the ant to crawl out of either the "Y" or "N" or accept whatever comes closest. (I've taken an "A" for "No"; a "Z" has stood for "Yes.") The questions tend not to be serious, because—even to myself—I prefer not to appear insane. Primarily I've been asking: What should we have for dinner? Should I attend this party in Irvine or this one, farther away, in Highland Park? I've been asking: Am I a good-enough person, yes or no?

July 4

On the Fourth of July, Uncle John forgets the ice. The fridge is full of food—broccoli and things that are not broccoli—and everyone is too lazy to drive to the store, so our sparkling lemonade stays warm. We watch fireworks from lawn chairs in the backyard. The highlights include a smiley-face firework—the eyes first burst together, then the mouth—and a green-and-gold firework that looks like a palm tree—green on the outside like leaves, gold on the inside like a trunk.

Hungry again later that night, we eat the hot dogs cold and without buns because we've run out, and we wipe the grease on Dad's stained old apron that says BOSS OF THE SAUCE.

Theo and I clink our warm lemonades together, then our cold hot dogs.

"Do you have a picture of her on your phone?" I ask.

"Who?" he says.

"The most severe," I say.

"Only if you show me yours."

"Deal."

Theo goes first. It's a close-up, taken by Theo; their faces and happiness fill the frame. They were camping, it looks like. Behind them I can make out their sleeping bags, pushed very close together, and only one pillow: one of those long, king-size ones, they were sharing. The photo was taken during a week they spent in Yosemite.

On a night, during that trip, they forgot to throw their food out, and a bear came to their tent.

"We thought this was it, we were going to die," Theo said.

"We made a promise that if we made it out alive, things would change."

She'd whispered, *I give you my word.* They had held hands and said they loved each other.

"This happened in the span of, like, a minute," Theo says.

A moment later the bear looked at them and ambled away, wholly uninterested.

The photo I have is from a vacation Joel and I took to Florida. We rented a car and we drove from Connecticut to Key West. We were squinting in the sunlight. At one of the rest stops he had second thoughts about leaving my iPod exposed so he put a receipt over it, like that would deter thieves.

We were celebrating the job Joel had gotten; in Miami we splurged on an expensive hotel, with walls so white they hurt to look at directly. The hotel had a pillow menu. From the hotel window we could see the small brown people stretched out on the sand like iguanas, and even smaller, the actual iguanas.

Our photos aren't so different—just some happy couple-ness.

I detect something like pride in Theo's voice, talking about her. It's not overt, but it's there. I notice the pride because, talking about Joel, I can hear the disappointment in my own.

She is very pretty, though, I think later.

Who cares, who cares, who cares, I chase the thought.

Even though I know it will give me nightmares, lately I can't stop searching the Internet for "feral goldfish." They have huge bubbly faces. What happens is people flush their goldfish, presumed dead, down the toilets. They get into the waterways and grow and grow and grow—sometimes to the size of soccer balls, according to these photographs.

"DAD," I shout. "COME HERE."

"Is it important?"

"Very!"

And he knows from my voice that I want to show him an enormous fish with a huge bubbly face. I do.

"You're a monster," he says, pleasantly. "Let's see it."

This one was fished out of a lake north of Detroit. The fisherman is holding the body and his young son, in tears, is holding on to an enormous fin like it's his mother's dress. The fish itself has its translucent eyelids hanging down, and it looks to be asleep. I hope it is.

And now, as of today, I'm thirty-one years old.

As a birthday present to myself I sneak onto campus, into Levin's office, and glue the caps to all of the prick's pens. I consider what else I can do that won't get me arrested. I've brought birthday gin with me to campus. It's in a clear plastic water bottle, an homage to my father. I'm using one of those dwarf bottles, which—under ordinary circumstances—I consider wasteful and absurd. Now I'm throwing bills maniacally into the fountain outside the Life Sciences building. Students going to their summer classes pick up their paces and hold their books closer.

"Ruth," I hear, about ten dollars later. It's Theo. He's walking toward me, holding something that looks like a deck of cards. As he approaches, I see that it's an ice-cream sandwich.

"That's a wish you want badly," he says, noticing all the paper money, afloat. He looks all around us, like he's looking for the money tree that dropped its leaves. He sits down, finishes the sandwich in a few solemn bites, and stands up to throw the wrapper away. When he sits back down, he sits closer, points to the bottle, and says, "May I?"

I shrug and hand him the bottle. He takes it.

I knew it started being over with Joel when I'd open a bottle of wine and he wouldn't drink it.

Sharing things is how things get started, and not sharing things is how they end. Theo is looking nicer than usual, I think, but then again, I'm drunk. Thoughts are springing to mind, and I am dropping them all, irresponsibly, like dice.

"So what's the wish?" he says, finally.

"Won't come true," I say.

"We both know you don't believe that," he says, observantly and correctly.

And because I am not going to make the same mistake I had when I was a kid, making those thousand wishes with Bonnie, all of them lost now, I decide not to keep it to myself. I have him lean over so I can whisper it. He smells like a delicious dryer sheet.

"What brand of dryer sheet is that?" I ask.

"Snuggle," he says, inching closer.

"Bullshit," I say. I inch back.

"Seriously," he says. "It's new. It's supposed to smell like apricots."

"You do smell like fruit," I say. I think he takes it as some kind of punch line, because immediately after that he kisses me. Immediately after which, I panic.

"I better go," I say, and stand up and flee.

"You're drunk?" Linus says, right away, on the phone. "Already? Without me?"

"Cut it out. Could you come get me?"

When the car pulls up to the curb and I get inside, Linus, without a word, tosses me a soft package, wrapped in HAPPY BIRTHDAY paper. The remainder of the tube of gift wrap is in the backseat.

Inside there are four pairs of socks, quality socks that haven't come from the dollar store, socks without type on the toes. He's rolled them into sock balls.

At home, my mother has laid out one of her mother's dresses, a gift for me, and my father has finally conceded that old journal of his. *Happy birthday, Ruth*, the Post-it affixed to it says.

Another Post-it opens to this page:

> *Today you asked why it was that people say*
> *cloudless but not cloudful. Today you made clear*
> *you did not know there was a difference in the*
> *spellings of "pitchers" and "pictures." You scraped*
> *seeds off of bagels and planted them in the flower*
> *bed out front. I didn't have the heart to tell you*
> *that there's no such thing as a bagel tree. Today*
> *I thought: I'm nuts—I'm just nuts—about you.*

July 10

Something else I appreciate about hangovers: you are given the chance to value your regular things. Water, for instance, becomes so delicious and appealing.

I like also that having a terrible day pretty much guarantees that the next day will be much, much better.

"Ruth," says the voice on our machine. It's Theo. "Call me, would you?"

At the café, there are pastries in the display case—croissants and bagels and bear claws—that look like uncomfortable people in a waiting room, trapped under bad fluorescent lighting.

The man in line in front of me orders a "small nonfat cap."

A woman orders a salad, rudely.

"Hello, shorty," says a lady to a dachshund outside the café door. "Hello!"

I have a staring contest with a gazing baby, and the way the baby, a fellow born human, looks at me it's like he is seeing a deep hidden thing that all the grown people can't. I look away first.

I won't call Theo. Because here's what I figure.

One of us could say: That was a mistake.

One of us could say: I like you.

One of us could say: I was drunk. Let's please forget it ever happened.

The other person could agree or disagree. The other person could waffle.

We could say these things, but what would be the point?

If it's presumptuous of me to think, at some future point, things won't work out, then, yes, I am being presumptuous.

Better presumptuous, I think, than a fucking sucker.

Because I'm through doing things that don't count. I'm through with things that don't *add up* or *amount.* I'm just through.

What Dad wrote:

> *Today I made you pancakes the shape of Mickey Mouse and you said NO, it was a butterfly. It had a fat body and small wings.*
>
> *Today you asked me what does "seduce" mean? S-e-d-u-c-e? What does it mean?*

Today you bit off the corners of your sandwich and announced you were taking the edge off.

Today you pronounced "worse" to rhyme with "horse."

Today I didn't catch you before you swallowed your chewing gum. I looked away for a second and then it was gone. I'm sorry.

Today was your birthday, and when it was time for you to blow out the candles, you wouldn't. Time was running out and you were anxious about it.

I don't know what to wish for, you told me sadly, after the candles had burned down to nothing.

That's okay, I told you. We put new ones in, and you successfully blew out this new set.

Today you mixed pretend Bloody Marys and used Scrabble tile holders for make-believe celery. It reminded me: I don't not have a drinking problem.

Today you put sand in the microwave. You said you were making glass.

Today you called your grandmother "small mom."

Today we walked past a café's colorful chalkboard and you asked me, "Why is that sun wearing a bra on his face?"

"Those are sunglasses," I told you.

Today we read aloud together and you pronounced "union" like "onion." A more perfect

onion. You read "apply" like it was about apples.
You are so happy to be learning to read.

Today I thought of what I would give to have
time just stop here. You're out of my league. I'm
waiting for the day you're going to leave me.

I'd give:

All the money I've got. My entire set of teeth.
That special silver dollar your grandfather gave me
and said would be worth $300,000 by the time you
were in college. Any of it, all of it, just to keep you
here.

July 11

Today Dad says—about the last sizes of lumber he needs—
could you write it all down, so I won't forget?

Write it all down, is what he says.

Okay, Dad, I say, and do:

This morning Mom was making a sandwich and you said,
Swiss cheese holes are called eyes. Your cheese watches you.

Today I cooked salmon and you said it was esculent.

Today you're wearing your old glasses, with the old prescription.

. . .

Today you tried that old trick you used to do. You would uncap beer with a single sheet of paper. You attempted it today with a bottle of ginger ale but couldn't manage. Today I wished that you had taught me.

Today you said, "I'm shitting bubbles. What could it mean?"

I'm no expert, so I called to make the appointment with Dr. Lung. We were all set to go, until I remembered that I'd dropped the remainder of the bar of soap into the toilet, by accident.

"You'll be okay, Dad," I told you, "and here's why."

Today you sliced into an onion that looked like Batman.

Today you said the sunshine was a stick of butter. "You could cut through that with a knife," you said.

Tonight I peeled peaches and we sat beneath the mostly done pergola, and in the moonlight your face was tired and lined like the underside of a cabbage leaf and I wondered what I looked like to you.

Today you wandered to the park, and I found you sitting on the sloping part of the hill, in the clover blossoms, eating from a big bag of *chicharrónes* and drinking a Coke and watching kids on the diamond throw a ball around. The vendor had wheeled his cart right up beside you, keeping an eye out, like a stealthy babysitter. He gave me a small nod when I approached, handed me a Coke to match yours.

"How long has he been here?" I asked—meaning you, how long had you been here—but the vendor only shrugged, as if to say, not to worry, it had been no trouble at all.

When I sat down beside you, we clinked our Cokes together; you handed me a *chicharrón*. We watched the kids. You mentioned that there were some things on your mind, but lately you were having trouble getting to them—accessing them. You had the feeling that all the thoughts were in a box covered in tape, and the trouble was there was too much tape, and the trouble was you didn't have the proper tools to access them—no scissors and no knife—and it was a lot of trouble—every day it was new trouble—trying to find the end of the tape.

You told me that in your twenties you had not believed in God, and for a little while you believed in sit-ups and eating right and meditation, and for a time after that you believed in *me* and Linus and my mother, and here you were, now, unable to open a box that had been taped shut, a box belonging to you.

Here you were. Here we both were.

You were saying all this, and even as you were saying it, I was trying to figure out how I'd respond when you asked, "Remind me. What kind of ball is that?"

I waited for you to say you were joking, and when you didn't, I said, "That's a baseball, Dad."

"Baseball," you repeated.

"Baseball gloves," I said. "Baseball bat, baseball diamond."

"Gloves, bat, diamond," you repeated, like this was a game, like this was *rock, paper, scissors*.

August

Today you washed your shoelaces.

Today you spoon-fed the neighbor's cat tuna from a can.

You've been eating the bananas too early, the ones that are spotless and still tinged green. I've taken to hiding a few from each bunch in the seat of the piano bench, but as of just now you've located this secret banana stash.

"Annie!" you marveled to Mom. "There's fruit inside this seat!"

Today I cooked clams, which I'd never done before. I read you're supposed to put them in water and throw in a handful of cornmeal, to encourage them to spit out their dirt, was what I read. The clams spat and spat, coughing, like they were afflicted with tiny clam colds.

Today you disappeared again, and scared the shit out of us.

This morning, when I called into your study, ready to hand you a mug of coffee, you didn't answer. I knocked, and when I opened the door you weren't there. Linus and I walked once around the block, then twice. I called Mom and told her not to panic, but she did. She found a substitute for herself, the substitute. We drove around and around and around the neighborhood, yelling HOWARD and DAD and not seeing you anywhere. We did this for three hours, so scared.

We would get home and call the police, we thought. But when we got home, there you were. We didn't know whether to be angry or to be relieved. Your nails had been painted silver. Your nails caught the light and they sparkled.

Today Mom brought home a heavy melon. You could smell how sweet it was from the outside, which was cracked. We each ate a quarter of a melon.

It was my first in years, because Joel couldn't stand cantaloupe.

Cantaloupe—it's delicious. I'd forgotten.

Today you told me that the Santa Ana winds are sometimes called the "devil winds." When they blow, the police department reports increases in domestic abuse and homicides. On TV, we see fires tearing over hills, fueled by dried-out vegetation.

At home, a confused wren throws its body, over and over, against the kitchen window. He sits on the sill, casts a puzzled glance, and tries again and again.

You blamed the wind. Linus and I drew straws to see which of us would deal with the body. It was like a toy, it was so small.

This morning Bonnie called to tell me about a fight she got into with Vince, and she said, "I blame the moon and the margaritas." The moon was full and planetary forces were in opposition, bringing confrontation to relationships, she said.

. . .

When the earthquake came it was 5.2 on the Richter scale. But you seemed not to even notice, like we were on a flight and simply experiencing regular turbulence. The epicenter was Brea. There were aftershocks for a week, and then nothing.

Whether the moon or the margaritas, Vince broke up with Bonnie last week, for inarticulate reasons, and she was quietly mourning. This was what, she said, she had wanted all along—but still.

On a Sunday, I surprised her at her apartment. Bonnie was in her glasses and pajamas. She had lopped her own hair into the tiniest pixie cut and looked striking. She yawned opening the door.

"Let's go," I said.

She got in the car and I drove. Outside it was hot, one hundred degrees at least, maybe more. We refilled our bottles with water from gas station bathrooms. In one of the bathrooms, a woman was hand-feeding her rabbit, through the grating on a cat carrier. At one of the gas stations, Bonnie filled her water bottle with blue slushie.

We stopped in Hadley for date shakes and, in Palm Springs, we checked into a motel that was supposedly a former mission. We watched the Home Shopping Network and thought about spending all our money on tennis bracelets because it was true, they looked very pretty in the studio lighting.

When I was little I thought that tennis bracelets were called tennis bracelets because the average wrist was the circumference of a tennis ball. Even while believing it, I had the feeling that it wasn't true. The saleswoman on the television now explained that in 1987, the tennis player Chris Evert was wearing a diamond bracelet, and in the middle of the match the bracelet broke, and they stopped the game so all of the diamonds could be recovered.

When the sun came up in the morning we saw our sunburned arms more clearly: my left and Bonnie's right. When I pressed her arm it turned white. I pressed "HI" and watched it fade. She pressed a sad face.

"What's a hairdresser's favorite herb?" I said.

"I don't know. What?"

"Cilantro."

"What?"

"It's in how you say it. Salon-tro."

"Ha ha," she said finally, and smiled for me.

We had written swear words on the dirty car and on the drive back the sun shone in a lovely way through the clear-lettered swears.

Today you and I sanded the patio. We each had hand sanders going, to cover ground faster. We're wearing goggles and earplugs and when Mom shouted at us about dinner we didn't hear it or see her. We sanded it down and then we wiped off the sawdust with tack cloth and our hands were still sticky when we ate dinner. They stuck to our forks. We shook our hands and they stuck.

Today was so hot that Bonnie, Linus, and I found the old kiddie pool, rinsed it out with the hose, and sat together in just our swim bottoms in the cold, shallow water until it warmed, at which point we'd top ourselves off with more cold water from the hose. Dad was out with Theo, and Bonnie had brought contraband vodka, so we mixed Kool-Aid with the vodka in a big thermos. Our mission was to drink it all, destroy the evidence.

After that we climbed the ladder to the top of Dad's half-painted patio cover, and lay on our backs to dry, on the partially pink slats. Bonnie curled up next to Linus, who was propped drowsily on an elbow, clutching, in his free hand, the bulb of his Kool-Aid–filled wineglass.

It had reached the point in the day when Linus started talking about teleportation. It was what he always wound up talking about after a certain number of drinks. I always wound up talking about whales. An amazing thing I can't really get over is that their shit isn't solid, but *liquid*. Also it's nutritious.

"Another weird thing is that pigs don't get milked," I said. "We don't have pig milk."

"Because piglets drink it all?" Bonnie said.

"Because piglets drink it all."

"There's something beautiful about that," Linus said, "beautiful and perfect."

We toasted to piglets and didn't notice Theo approach.

"What's happening up there?" he yelled, startling Linus, who nearly fell off.

"Who are you?" Bonnie called, at first. Then, deciding she didn't care, she said, "Drink the Kool-Aid!"

Of course I said nothing, like an idiot. My fear was a bratwurst: sobering.

"How was the Home Depot?" asked Linus. You had wanted to spend a gift card.

"He bought one of those pots that boils water."

"Isn't that what all pots do?"

"The kind that plugs in, you know. To the wall."

"Hey, the blonde the other day," Bonnie said, all of a sudden. "Who's she? They looked like chums, she and your dad."

When had she seen Joan, I wondered?

"Don't you mean," I said, "that *she* looked like chum, the chopped fish and fish oils dumped overboard to attract fish?"

"I give it six years, swear to God," Linus said. "Teleportation. I'm willing to bet on this."

"I better go," Theo said.

"Don't leave," Bonnie said.

"I better go," he said again, and he went.

Today Theo came to pick you up to watch the game and grab a bite and while you were fetching your things we stood at the door making very, very small talk.

You were taking your sweet time. There was an aftershock just then. It helped—it was something to talk about.

Today we planted pumpkins and squash in the garden. We ate too many figs from the tree and it made us giddy and our hearts beat fast, like we'd drunk too much coffee. All summer we've been trying to get a handle on the cheatgrass in the yard. Some things you try to fight and others you have to let defeat you, I guess is the thing. I gave up on birdseed. I filled the feeder with plums and let the scrub jays have at it.

. . .

I've been having the same dream every night this week—a dream serialized. It picks up, every night, where it left off the night before. It must have something to do with the heat.

In the dream, we are all together—you, Mom, Linus, me—living in a big house. We have pets. We have fifty-eight dogs, all types and breeds. You feed them and you care for them and you are yourself again; you can remember everything.

The first night, the first dream, a Labrador runs away, and you are so upset. In the dream we go looking for her; we post signs around the neighborhood. But she's nowhere to be found; she's gone for good. And we notice that you have forgotten the past year's events. After that it's a dachshund, and then a poodle. And the more dogs that run away, the more you forget.

Finally, we realize what's been happening. You've been using the dogs as mnemonic devices to recall whole years. You were connecting eyes and ears to specific feelings or events of a given twelve months; a baseball game to a shade of pupil, a fishing trip to a puppy's nail. After ten dogs run away you can't remember anything from the past ten years. And then it's fifteen. And then you forget Linus. And then you forget me.

Mom can know without counting when there are thirty dogs left. She can recognize you at age thirty, when you first met: flirting, earnest, trying so hard to impress her.

Last night I dreamt that there were six dogs left. In the dream, you sat on the floor running your hands over a retriever the color of pale hay.

• • •

Today you said, Did you know that we share fifty percent of our DNA with bananas?

Men share fifty-one, Mom said, deadpan, not looking up.

We looked at each other. A dick joke!

Today you, Linus, and I finished painting the patio cover pink to match the house.

"That wasn't so bad, right?" I asked you.

"Well, no," you said, surveying your work. "But it isn't so good."

And Linus, covered in pink, started to laugh. Then you, then me—all of us, pink and laughing, like lunatics.

September

Today I cooked you spaghetti and the sauce tasted plain and sour. Sugar and fat are bad for you. I didn't want to include anything bad.

But today you said, Think of all the mice the scientists are studying: all those mice with Alzheimer's. What do they forget? They forget many things, but they never forget how much they like peanut butter.

Okay, I said. Okay, okay, okay, and added more butter and a little sugar to the sauce, which made it much better.

. . .

Today we drove to the beach. We sat in the sand and ate pretzels and drank lemonade from a stand. A dog and his owner were standing nearby. The owner was holding a tube of new-looking tennis balls. He pitched one toward the surf, and said, very enthusiastically, "Thousand, go get it, boy!" and when the dog stayed put he looked truly crestfallen. "Aw, Thousand," he said, "you fucking suck-ass bitch."

On the way home, we stopped at the coin-operated car wash. We had a plan. I put the quarters in—two dollars for five minutes—and you scrubbed with the scrub brush while I held the hose and sprayed it down. When we vacuumed the seats we found a hundred-dollar bill, and on the way home we debated how to spend it.

Today Theo came to pick you up—the two of you were getting coffees—and mumbled hello, like a teenage boy there to pick up his date. Hello, I tried to say coolly and responsibly, like a parent.

Today you asked about my job at the hospital. I'd always thought you were uninterested—disappointed, even, at what I'd chosen. An ultrasound measures the speed of sound as it passes through different substances in the body, I told you.

I told you about what I did for a living: how I scanned people's bodies, and took pictures of their soft tissues. How I

liked breaking the news to couples who were having twins, seeing the shock and then excitement—or the horror.

There was a day, in that month before I left, I watched
Grooms give an echocardiogram, and she showed me this new
equipment that could isolate a heart. Any organ, you could isolate. With this program you could see whatever organ float as
though in space.

Later, when I steeled a patient for her tracheotomy, and held
a clubfooted baby for his tired mother, I thought about that
heart, alone and spinning.

Today you were sitting in front of the computer. An actor's face
was tiled on the screen. Later, on the same computer, I saw the
tabs you had open. Searches for *electricity* and *Berlin* and *memory
improvement.*

An hour today, you spent shouting. You said we'd stolen money
from you. You threw your pillows over the fence and into the
Grovers' pool. You broke the legs off of your dining table chair.
You smashed almost all of our drinking glasses.

In a matter of days, Lung had said, it can go from being manageable to scary.

And after you'd frightened us all completely, you sat in the living room and quietly ate a banana you found in the piano bench.
And after that, you wept.

• • •

You said you were sorry, after that. You said you wanted to help. You said you wanted to help us get ready, for when things would be worse.

We wrapped everything breakable. All of Mom's favorite colored glasses we wrapped in newspaper and put away. We hid the knives. We picked out colorful plastic tumblers at the store.

Two sets of doorknobs was your idea. For the front and back doors, working doorknobs lower. There's a knob in the regular position, one that doesn't turn—you can't actually turn the knob to get out of the house. The functional knob would be lower on the door, near our ankles.

Trying the knob located in the regular position, you'll assume the door is broken, and this will deter you from leaving. When things get worse, that is.

Today we marked handles and the light switches with red nail polish.

Today we separated everyone's dark and white clothes, as though for an enormous load of laundry. All the darks, we donated to the Goodwill.

It was on the forum where I had read: dark colors can appear threatening to the patient with dementia. Black clothing can cause anxiety. If you put a black rug on the floor, an individual in the disease's later stages will be afraid to step over it, for fear that it is a hole.

. . .

Today you held your open hand out and I shook the pills into it, same as every day. Fish oil. Magnesium. Vitamins D and C and A. Gingko biloba.

"Hello, water," you said, holding the glass against the moonlight and shaking the pills, like they were dice you were ready to roll, in your other hand. "Goodbye, vitamin."

We bought nightlights, because darkness—lack of sunlight—causes confusion and disorientation. The increased agitation and anxiety is called *sundowning*. Lung recommended that we keep a light on at all times.

I tried using the nightlight in my room but quit: I couldn't fall asleep.

Someone on the online forum also said: Imagine you are preparing the home for an inquisitive child. We looked at a childproofing list. We put away anything you could choke on. You described the process of childproofing the house for me: how I would stagger around like a small drunk person, making loud and confident proclamations.

Today, buying refills of vitamins, I bought two of each type, so from now on, I can take them with you.

Today we cooked dinner. We baked a "hummingbird cake" for dessert: pecan halves on the top. Various spices. Why hummingbird? You asked the question, but we didn't bother to look it up, just because.

We've locked away the scissors and the knives in a drawer using one of those plastic childproof locks.

No more poisonous plants, in case you decide, down the line, to eat them. We got rid of everything inedible. We posted emergency numbers to the refrigerator: doctor, police, fire department, the Poison Control Center.

Today I applied for sonography certification. It's a two-year program. When it's through I can be a cardiac sonographer.

Today I found an almond with a slight curve and I didn't eat it. I found another nut with a curve. I put the two anomalous nuts into a jar. Because, well, what can I do?

October

Today I looked glum, I guess, and you told me it was perfectly normal. "It's called 'the fall,' my love," you said.

Today we ate grapes from a mug and met a white dog that looked like David Bowie.

. . .

Today we watched something on PBS about the evolution that's happening right now, right under our noses. Cliff swallows in Nebraska are evolving shorter wings so as not to be hit and killed by cars. Otter penis bones are shrinking because of pollutants in English and Welsh rivers. Earlier I'd stepped on a coffee cup lid and liked it, then thought, *What if, someday, we evolve to like the crunch of coffee cup tops more than leaves? And the streets just stay filled with them?*

Today we went for a run together, at the high school track. Though it makes no sense, you're in better shape than me. You lapped me handily, pumping your fist as you did.

Today Theo came over with a six-pack of root beer and chicken taquitos and Monopoly. We spent four hours as a hat, boot, terrier, and thimble, which Theo wanted but let me have. You bought Boardwalk and Park Place, and Theo accumulated property after inexpensive property, while I languished in jail, seemingly forever. It was Linus who won, in his quiet, diligent way.

After he left you said, I'm senile but I'm not blind.
   What? I said.
   That wasn't so bad, was it? you said.

Today at the store you stole a chicken, by mistake. What happened was we lost each other at the store, and after I had paid for our things, I found you outside, clutching this chicken like it belonged to you—like it was your motorcycle helmet. I knew immediately it was theft: you hadn't brought your wallet with you.

What do we do? I said, panicked, and you shushed me, and we walked, briskly, to the car.

We should bring it back, I said, at home later.

Don't be ridiculous, you said, and we put it into our Ronco rotisserie.

Today we went to the Boomers! that used to be a Family Fun Center, that used to be a Bullwinkle's. We played skee ball. We ate a funnel cake. We shook hands with a man in a dirty moose costume. We sat in a photo booth and a few minutes later it spat out a strip of photos of us.

Today we went to the pumpkin patch—the same patch where, when I was seven, a pumpkin farmer reprimanded me for picking one up by its stem. That same farmer was there today; he still looked dour.

All the pumpkins were $4.99, regardless of their size.

You picked out a small pale white pumpkin and I chose one in regular orange, with the longest, most twisted stem. At home we carved the faces, and you told me mine was familiar. That makes no sense, I argued with you.

· · ·

Later you rummaged in a shoe box until you found it: a photo of me, seven years old, grinning stupidly with a pumpkin I'd just carved. It was this pumpkin's twin, with an identical face.

Today I found an avocado skin on the dish rack, like a drying dish.

Today I saw you and Mom in the living room, reading, sitting very close. My foot fell asleep, you said to her. You took her hand and placed it on your foot and asked Mom, Can you feel it, tingling?

November

Today a court summons came in the mail for me. I don't know how they managed to find me. On Monday, I'm supposed to show up for jury duty.

"The word *testify*," you said, "comes from testicles. Men used to swear by their balls."

Today Mom told me that she ate apples during both pregnancies because she heard it'd keep Linus and me from having asthma. You'd shave the wax off them with a butter knife, was what she told us when we asked about it—because earlier we had watched you diligently shave the wax off a Pippin apple.

• • •

I'd picked my phone up without noticing who it was, and the voice asked how you were, and the voice belonged to Joel. Now we were having a conversation. I was in the grocery store. I was staring at a pink pyramid of foreign tomatoes.

I said you were good and he said, That's good.
He said, Tell him I say hi. Tell your mom hi, too.
(Joel says hi. This is how I'm telling you.)

The next thing he said was, I'm getting married.
Congratulations, I said, the way people do.
Kristin is actually pregnant, he admitted.
Congratulations! I said again, and asked how she was,
    and how far along.
It's scary, he laughed. It's exciting.

I had an idea of what was coming, what was inevitable: in no time at all I would feel bereft and intractable. Joel's getting married, I could handle, but Joel's making a new human with Kristin, for some reason, I couldn't. Bonnie was on vacation, in Mexico, with her parents. I dialed Theo.
    "Hello," I said.
    "Hi there," he said.
    "What do you say to a night of heavy drinking?"
    "What's the occasion?" Theo asked.
    "Oh," I said. "No reason."

"I don't believe you," he said. I could tell he was smiling. "But I accept."

"On one condition," he added.

"Anything," I said.

"No getting sad-drunk," he said, very seriously.

"I won't," I said, just as seriously.

We met at Nelly's downtown, where you used to like to go, I know. While I stood by the bar, waiting for Theo, a man asked if I was Chelsea, and another man asked if I was Audrey.

"Why is that?" I asked, when Theo showed up.

"It's a popular spot," he explained, "for blind dates."

This was because there weren't many watering holes to choose from in town. Theo pointed out the regulars. There was a man who looked like Hemingway. Theo said he's been there ever since the day he outlived his wife. Whenever he is here, he buys two drinks, one for her, which he intends not to drink. The first he drinks slowly, but in the end he can't bear to let the second go to waste. He always drinks them both.

There was a man named Joseph, who spent years in prison, and in that time had managed to loosen and ultimately extricate one eye with a coffee stirrer. His left eye, because he'd heard about the heightened senses of the blind and wanted to better hear his heart, in case it ever stopped.

There was Leonard, who—after a few drinks—will stand on the bench outside throwing a cotton sheet into the air, trying to catch some old ghost.

"With a bedsheet?" I asked.

"You have a better idea?" Theo said.

What Leonard figures is that a ghost is something like wind, and the sheet will catch the shape.

"It's not about catching, like a trap," Theo explained. "More like capturing, like a photograph."

Leonard sipped quietly at something that resembled a Shirley Temple, stood, and fed several quarters into the jukebox. His selection, it turned out, was "Blue Bayou."

Somebody was telling his friend, in a conspiratorial way, "Listen, Louie. You're never gonna see your name in lights unless you change your name to Exit!"

There was a couple who looked to be on a date, with numerous empty and uncollected glasses in front of them. The woman was fishing the lime out of the man's drink, dropping it into the clear contents of her own cup. A way of flirting, I guess.

"You're so pretty for no reason," the man said, thoughtfully. He said it like he was proud to have arrived at that insight.

"Don't get drunk," Theo said all of a sudden, noticing me. He held my gaze. "Don't get drunk, Ruth."

And then to take my mind off what he knew it had troublingly rested on he started rattling off trivia.

He asked me did I know that, when you get a kidney transplant, they leave your original kidneys in your body? The third kidney goes in your pelvis.

He asked did I know that it rains diamonds on Jupiter? Did I know that Russia is bigger than Pluto?

And I asked did he know that Robert Kearns, inventor of

the intermittent windshield wiper, was blind in one eye from a champagne cork on his wedding night? And Theo said yes, for whatever reason he did happen to know that, and did I know that he was tangled up in patent infringement lawsuits with Ford and Chrysler, because after Kearns had tried to sell the technology to them, they installed his wipers anyway?

He won against Ford and Chrysler but lost against GM and Mercedes. His wife, Phyllis, whom he had married that champagne-cork night, ultimately left him because all the litigation got to be too taxing.

He explained that he had trouble sleeping through the night—he woke up in the middle of the night, almost every night. The trick was not forcing yourself to go back to sleep. The trick was to eat a bowl of cereal, go on the Internet, and read list after list of facts, until you're lulled into something like sleep.

All of a sudden Joseph materialized in front of us.

"She's Howard's kid?" he said to Theo.

"I am," I said.

"There's a resemblance," he said to me. "Tell your dad Joseph says hi."

By the jukebox Leonard was repeating "I'm awed" or maybe "I'm odd," over and over.

"I'm selfish," I started to say. I stopped, realizing that saying so was, itself, pretty selfish. I hung my head.

I remembered the time Joel and I had met after work to have a couple of drinks at the bar down the street, and how we'd meant to stop by for only happy hour, and how we wound up playing pool until midnight—how, outside the bar, a man was standing with a cardboard sign that said: WAKE UP, YOU DRUNK-

ARDS, AND WEEP. This was attributed to the Bible, Joel 1:5—
how hilarious and how appropriate it had seemed then.

When I brought it up, months later, Joel said, "What are
you talking about?" because he didn't remember it—he'd forgotten it completely—and it was at that point I realized that I
could remember something and he could remember something
different and if we built up a store of separate memories, how
would that work, and would it be okay? The answer, of course,
in the end, was no.

"That's not allowed," Theo said. "Despair's off-limits. That
was the condition, remember?"

"I don't know," I said. "What do we do instead?"

"Instead," he said, like he was really considering the question, "basketball."

Another couple was outside the bar. "We had a time." The man
was agreeing to something or other the woman had said, a
smoke in his hand. She seemed distraught. He'd taken a drag
and blown, so they looked to be cocooned in smoke.

"But times end," the man was saying. "Even the good ones.
Especially the good ones. That's what they do."

Everybody everywhere, I think, is always talking about the
same shitty thing.

We made our way to the park. Officially, it was closed. Unof-
ficially, there wasn't anybody around to enforce the rule. We
stopped at the Shell station, on the way, and picked up a six-
pack of those skinny cans of sugary black coffee. We played
Horse first, then one-on-one. I knew he expected me to be

terrible. Everyone does. I look like the sort of girl who throws like a girl. But I can play basketball because you taught me. I like to surprise people with that.

We played until the coffee ran out. We sat on a bench—just sat—and watched the sun light up the sky over the mountains. We sat close because we had no choice: the other half of the bench was covered in bird shit. He didn't try anything and I didn't try anything, and we only sat, without thoughts, tired and colder than we wanted to admit was comfortable. It was, I admit, *nice*. It felt like a stupid movie, and I knew I would waste all of the next day sleeping to make up for it, and all of a sudden I hated that word, *waste*; wished it didn't exist; wished I'd been braver on so many long-gone occasions; wished things were not as they were.

Why don't we get married? was how Joel had proposed.

"Why don't we?" he liked to say. What a chickenshit way to say things.

"I don't believe you," I said to Theo.

"What?"

"About the kidneys," I said.

I texted Grooms to see if it was true and even though it was who knows what time, she texted back, immediately, that it was.

"What else don't I know?" I said, and Theo grinned.

The sun had come up fully by now, and he squinted—smiled.

We walked to his car. There were sweet gum leaves stuck to it—the dew had affixed them like glue. The leaves were beautiful, the color of Fanta. He opened the door and on the way home we listened to the soft-rock station, which was already playing Christmas songs. Theo sang along to "Little Drummer Boy."

At home you were reading the newspaper and eating a pancake with your hands, dipping it into the syrup.

This week a poster showed up on our street, describing a missing cat as "muscular." There was a bike handcuffed to the bike rack outside the post office. We watched a man throw a ball to his dog, who obediently fetched it. But the ball seemed to be getting smaller and smaller. When we came up close, we saw that the ball wasn't a ball at all, but a hard, round dinner roll.

Dr. Lung, today, didn't look happy or sad. He just *looked*.

There were pigeons wandering the parking lot of the medical center. They appeared lost, though of course they weren't. They're famously never lost. They're the type of birds that carry messages. The likelier explanation was that they were *hungry*. The birds, roving the lot, looked hungry.

"Let's go," I said.

I drove us back to the In-N-Out we'd passed on the way. I ordered two strawberry shakes and a box of fries, and handed one of the shakes to you. We sat on the curb and fed fries to pigeons. We saw Dr. Lung make his way to his parked car. It was a compact Japanese car that looked recently washed. At first, I almost didn't recognize him, because without the white coat he looked like anybody: someone's goofy cousin.

"This is a nice day," you said. I had been wondering if feeding the birds was jogging a memory for you. I had been preoccupied with wondering. There was a breeze and the breeze was carrying the smell of eucalyptus, and the day was cool but not too cool.

You repeated about how nice the day was, either because you really wanted me to know it or because you'd forgotten you already mentioned it, but all of a sudden, it didn't matter what you remembered or didn't, and the remembering—it occurred to me—was irrelevant. All that mattered was that the day was nice—was what it was.

Today we went to the bowling alley, where it turns out Sam still works and looks exactly the same, with hair the same color and shape as a Q-tip. He could still look at our feet and give us shoes in the exact sizes. You kept picking up the heaviest ball.

That one's too heavy, Dad, Linus and I kept saying.

It'll be fine, Mom said.

You bowled three strikes in a row and Mom did a happy dance. You were given a turkey—Thanksgiving dinner.

We've been trying to figure out why the Honeybell tree out front never used to produce any fruit but, this year, won't stop. Nobody has a satisfying explanation for why. Mom thinks rainfall and you keep insisting the tree's triumphed, finally, over a silent and murderous disease. I think it has to do with bees and their unknowable bee whims.

I like to watch insect specials when nothing good is on TV, and nothing ever is, anymore. There's a lot to admire about bees, I think. For one thing, they know exactly what to do in life—they have jobs and they do them. Also, they see life frame by frame, with those panels for eyes, like movie screens.

"They recognize *faces*," I told Mom.

"You're saying they missed you?" she joked.

I was in the kitchen when you approached. You cast a look of concern at the colander of cauliflower.

"No more crucified vegetables," you said.

"But they died for you, Dad."

"No more."

"Lasagna?"

"Lasagna," you agreed, and so I made a lasagna. The sauce we made with a sweet onion and sweet butter and pork that I braised. We ate it with big spoons, and no vegetables were sacrificed in the process.

While I was mopping the kitchen, a creature, winged, flew my way. After a few lame swats I propped the broom against the wall and decided to flee. I headed to Theo's.

"Can cockroaches fly?" I asked, when he opened the door.

"Is that why you're here?" He meant to sound exasperated, I knew, but he was grinning.

"It's looking good, this place," I said.

He patted his new couch, in the way somebody might

gingerly pat a stranger's dog, to indicate that I should have a seat. It was a nice couch, and I said so.

"But I'm no expert," I said.

"You're not?"

"Nope."

"What are you an expert in?"

"Nothing," I said. Then, after some consideration: "The fetal position."

"You're supposed to get into a fetal position during a bear attack, aren't you?" Theo said. "Because it indicates to the bear that you're not a threat?"

"The fetal position—exactly. And, get this, I know *all kinds*."

Last night Theo dropped by for dinner and afterward the five of us walked to the park, and then you, Mom, and Linus peeled off, citing exhaustion, so Theo and I sat on a bench by the water, trying to catch the comet that we'd been told, by the weatherman, was going to pass.

"That duck over there is having a drink," Theo said, pointing to the duck on the side of the pond, with his bill probing the mouth of a tallboy.

"What do you think that duck is going to do without inhibitions?"

"The real question is what inhibitions does that duck have in the first place?"

"No more flying south for the winter."

"No more Mr. Nice Duck. No more politely accepting stale bread from strangers."

"I'm more interested in the morning after. A duck's self-loathing."

"A duck's regret."

"Look," I said, cutting to the chase.

I told him I felt "generally positive" about him. He said he felt "generally positive" about me, too. He gave me an awkward hug and later I found that he'd put a peppermint in my jacket pocket.

Today, like a lot of days lately, you forget some names.

"The one I'm carrying a torch for," you said.

"Mom? Annie?" I said. "Are you talking about Annie?"

"That's the one," you said.

The mind tells you what or whom to love, and then you do it, but sometimes it doesn't: sometimes the mind plays tricks, and sometimes the mind is the worst. But I'm trying—I really am—not to think about those things.

In the garage, I found my rock tumbler. You and Mom gave it to me for Christmas years ago. Inside I found a smooth and beautiful misshapen pearl—one of my baby teeth, I remembered.

Today I gave you my old seashell collection. You arranged all the shells at the bottom of your fish tank in a pretty way.

"Thank you for the exoskeletons," you said to me.

"You're welcome," I said to you.

• • •

Today you and Linus both left for somewhere, and I don't know where you went or what you did, but when you came home you sat together on the couch and shared a Sprite.

Today was Thanksgiving. I stared stupidly at the turkey, not knowing what to do with it, even after spending the month in a sea of cookbooks on turkey preparation, on loan from the library. You would not believe the vastness of literature and debate over wet versus dry brine, stuffed versus unstuffed, breast-side up or down.

I cried uncle, my only uncle. I called John.

"The bigness is irrelevant," he said, sounding fed up. "Think of it as a large chicken."

But still John sacrificed his whole afternoon to help stud the ham with peppercorns, while—in the living room—you and Mom napped straight into the evening, her feet inside the bottoms of your pants.

Partway through dinner there was a knock on the door. I opened the door, and there was Grooms, looking coiffed and perfect as usual. She had Kevin in her arms and a crate of pears at her feet.

"Hi," she said.

I screamed, and hugged Grooms as hard as I thought I could without killing Kevin, who was between us.

She'd driven down, on the vague invitation to spend Thanksgiving with her ex-husband's family in Laguna Beach. Brady had said something cryptic to her about wanting to meet Kevin. The house was in a gated community; she gave Brady's sister's name to the security guard. She circled the house a few times, changed her mind, and headed here.

"I don't know what I was thinking," she said, sheepish.

"You're fine," I said, and ushered them in.

You and Mom took turns with Kevin in your laps, spooning him potato.

"He's so fat!" you exclaimed, happily. You bounced him on your knee.

Today you put a whole cabbage into our Ronco Showtime rotisserie.

Today, into the enormous salad I was making, you slam-dunked a whole tomato.

Today you took my hand and filed a nail, the way people do to babies.

Today, I caught you in the garage, eating the peaches from the earthquake kit. I joined you. We drank the syrup and then we drank the packets of water.

Here I am, in lieu of you, collecting the moments.

Collecting—I guess that's the operative word. Unless it's *moments*.

Linus—who still loves Christmas the most of any of us—did the decorating. He walked around and around all the trees in the front yard, winding each of them with Christmas lights. He spray-painted the oranges gold. He came home from the super-market with red and green candy corn—"reindeer corn," the packaging called it. He built a gingerbread house and tasked me with the job of applying the icing mortar. He bestowed, upon each of us, a brick-sized gift in snowman wrapping paper—wrapped so expertly and taped so excessively, it would be impos-sible to unwrap and rewrap the gift without detection.

You said, You'll be free to go soon.

You said, I'm still your father and I still make the rules around here.

And when I said, Sure, Dad, what are my rules? you said that after Christmas, you wanted me to leave. You didn't want me feeling obligated to stay. You said you didn't want me feel-ing guilty. You said you didn't want me seeing you act loony tunes. Loony tunes: that's what you said.

I told you that I would think about that rule. You said there was no thinking about it: you were my father, a rule is a rule. I told you I was a grown-ass woman, unfortunately, and didn't have to listen to you.

Theo and I went to a restaurant. A date, I guess, you could call it—and in fact you did, when you opened the front door. You whistled at us when I climbed into his car.

At the bistro, our server struggled to remember the pie list. Theo put glasses on to read the menu. We watched a waitress— who didn't think anyone was looking—down half-full beer glasses left by patrons. Later, we walked along a street that was remarkable in that it was completely unremarkable. There were no stores of any interest. There were two tanning salons. Theo took my hand and I didn't try to wrest it free.

"The cat's name was Fluffy," he said, and when I imagined Theo as a little boy getting his hand scratched up by a mean cat with an inappropriate name, my heart went insane.

Later that week there was Theo calling and Theo saying, "Look at the moon." Us sharing a bottle of bourbon he'd tucked into a mitten. Me saying, "How farsighted are you?" pulling him really, really, really close, so close that you could string a tight-rope tautly from his pupils to my pupils and an insect could tiptoe across it.

"What can you see?" I asked.

When he didn't answer right away, I flinched, a little.

"Enough," was what he said, finally. It might've been an insult. It felt like the correct answer.

There was a night, a few nights later, at his place, when he thought I was asleep, and said, "You're too perfect."

I knew I should protest; I had a list of reasons with which I could. I also knew I couldn't, because we'd both be embarrassed if I did.

• • •

This morning, we opened Linus's impeccably wrapped presents. He'd gotten each of us a walkie-talkie, which he'd labeled with our names.

You and Linus watched a Christmas movie marathon on TV, and Mom and I cooked dinner. We invited everyone: John and his girlfriend, Lisa, and the Nazaryans. Mom cooked the turkey and I helped with the hundred other things: a pecan pie with chocolate in it, two stuffings, macaroni and cheese, vegetables both cruciferous and not.

I made unsuccessful gingerbread men—the recipe was a stinker. Mom had always recommended eating the legs first, so your gingerbread men wouldn't run away. It's something I still do, I noticed yesterday, taking the legs off these bad cookies without a second thought.

Cleaning out my purse earlier in the week, I had found *Cookery by Carl*, the endive guy, and I made his recipe for boats: endive leaves and cheese and nuts and honey.

My earliest memory, I think, I've narrowed down to this. I'm two or three, maybe, I'm with you, in Riverside, in the one-bedroom apartment where you and Mom slept on the bottom bunk and me on the top.

In that same apartment, the next year, I caught pneumonia, remember? And you gave me a sponge bath? And my temperature rose and now I know the worry you probably had, the worry that I'd have brain damage.

Anyway, the memory: You are holding my hand. You're cutting my fingernails, and I'm crying, first because I'm expecting that the procedure will be painful, later because it doesn't meet my expectations: it feels like nothing, and the feeling of nothing is disorienting.

I remember your large hand, holding my small hand. Your being so careful to clip the nails off my tiny, tiny fingers. I remember that sponge bath, too, and how I was so scared the water would be too cold, but it wasn't—to my fevered body, it was just cool enough.

Theo arrived first, wearing a khaki shirt. He lingered at the threshold. I told him I liked his shirt. He said he had advice on it. He asked a waitress what he should wear on a date. She'd told him a khaki shirt.

"Is this a date?" I asked. "It's Christmas."

"It's never *not* worked," he said. A pause, and then he took my wrist and knocked my knuckles to the wooden door frame.

Next was Uncle John, with Lisa, then Bonnie with her parents and a macaroni salad heavy with mayonnaise.

John set up the bar, and for the rest of the night he played bartender, putting eggs into drinks: Golden Slippers, which are apricot brandy, chartreuse, and a yolk. The whites he saved for September Mornings: rum, brandy, lime juice, and grenadine. He was using real limes because he hated those squeeze bottles, and so a line was amassing for the drinks, out the kitchen and into the living room; John squeezed each lime individually, and one had to smile patiently if one wanted a good drink, because he was testy otherwise, as usual.

You carved the turkey and you carved the ham, and we drank John's cocktails and you binge-drank Shirley Temples and, Dad, you were making fun of Mom's affinity for reggae, which she blamed us for—she only got into it because we loved dancing to it, as babies—and Uncle John was talking angrily about his neighbors, who own cows, and Lisa was pushing her hand lightly on his arm as if to say, *Easy now*, and everybody was holding paper plates that were bending into parabolas with the weight of all the food.

And much later, after everybody is gone, and when it is just the four of us again, and we've dealt with all of the dishes, this is what you do: you turn the low doorknobs and we walk single file out the door, staying within sight of one another, in our light-colored clothes. "Testing, testing," Linus says, over a walkie-talkie. "Roger that," I respond. It's after midnight by now, meaning it isn't Christmas anymore. It's an ordinary, regular night—and I prefer it, to be honest. The moon is doing something beautiful. Mom's trailing you, clutching your little finger.

She pulls a peeled orange from her jacket pocket and hands it to Linus to distribute the segments.

"Mom's brought an orange, Dad," Linus says. "Do you copy?"

"I copy," you say, then "Over and out," and all of us follow your lead, one after the other, into the darkness: over and over and over. Out, out, out.

Acknowledgments

This book began in Gainesville, Florida, so I'll start there: Thank you to my teachers, Padgett Powell, David Leavitt, Jill Ciment, and Mary Robison. Thank you to my inimitable MFA@FLA cohort, especially Christina Nichol, Philip Pinch, David Blanton, Kate Sayre, James Davis, Kevin Hyde, Hai-Dang Phan, Harry Leeds, and Diya Chaudhuri. Thanks also, Terita Heath-Wlaz, for loaning me a Dante-ism, and Andrew Donovan for the two lovely words in sequence. I finished this book in San Francisco, but never would have were it not for the mornings spent at Charlie's with Mimi Lok. Thank you, Namwali Serpell for your early read and insight; thank you, Lauren Ro and Jessica Wang for your unwavering friendship and encouragement. Thank you, Dave Desmond, Daniel Roubian, and Ken Kirkeby in Diamond Bar, and John Crowley, J. D. McClatchy, and Caryl Phillips in New Haven.

Incommensurate thanks goes to Marya Spence and Sarah Bowlin for all of the things. I could not have lucked out any harder than with you brilliant two. Thank you to Barbara Jones, Kerry Cullen, Kanyin Ajayi, and everyone at Holt who did the magical work of turning this Word document into a book. I'm so very, very, very grateful.

Thank you to my parents, Edward and Lynn, for your unending and unconditional support, faith, sacrifice, and love. (This book is for you. Sorry for all the curse words.) Thank you to my brothers, Clement and Ben, for your cheerleading and good humor. Thank you to my grandmother, Chew-Lai Ping: We miss you. And thank you to Eli Horowitz: Your feedback was imperative and your love is even more so.